THE MYSTERY OF THE
MIDNIGHT MARAUDER

Trixie Belden

Your TRIXIE BELDEN Library

Trixie Belden and the
MYSTERY OF THE
MIDNIGHT MARAUDER

BY KATHRYN KENNY

Cover by Ben Otero

 **GOLDEN PRESS**
Western Publishing Company, Inc.
Racine, Wisconsin

CONTENTS

THE MYSTERY OF THE MIDNIGHT MARAUDER

Odd Behavior • 1

JEEPERS!" Trixie Belden exclaimed breathlessly as she hurried into the kitchen. "I've never walked so far in my entire life. It didn't do any good, either. I couldn't find Reddy anywhere. Did you two have any luck?"

She flung herself into the nearest chair and gazed at her older brothers inquiringly.

Brian looked up from his breakfast. "Hey, slow down, Trix," he said. "What's all this about Reddy? Isn't he outside? Did you call him?"

Trixie stared. "No, Reddy isn't outside—at least, not where he's supposed to be. And of course I called him. I've been calling him for the last half hour—and searching, too." She frowned. "So where were you?"

Mart, who had been pushing his scrambled eggs around on his plate with his fork, flushed guiltily. "Sorry, Trix," he mumbled. "I guess I forgot to give Brian your message."

Trixie gasped. "You forgot about *Reddy?*"

Mart avoided her eye. "I did say I was sorry. Anyway, this isn't the first time that dog's been gone all night. Reddy's probably chasing a rabbit through the woods or something."

Brian grinned with relief and relaxed against the back of his chair. "Sure," he agreed, "I'll bet that's what he's doing. If not, I expect he's over at Manor House with Honey. Did you think of looking there?"

Trixie bit back the sharp retort that sprang to her lips. She was a sturdy fourteen-year-old whose temper sometimes had a short fuse, though her blond curly hair and big blue eyes belied the fact.

Right now she was struggling to hold on to that temper. *After all*, she thought, *the boys couldn't be expected to know that I've just got back from Manor House.*

After searching the grounds of Crabapple Farm, which nestled in a green hollow not far from the Hudson River, it was only natural that Trixie should have thought next of the Wheelers' mansion. It stood high on the neighboring hill, just west of the Beldens' cozy farmhouse, where Trixie lived with her parents and three brothers—and Reddy.

Trixie knew that the lovable Irish setter enjoyed the Wheelers' huge estate as much as she did. He liked their stable full of horses and the private lake for swimming. He liked the game preserve and the woods, which were deep, dark, and mysterious, with trails that crossed and recrossed each other.

And he particularly liked Honey Wheeler, who was the same age as Trixie, and who had been Trixie's best friend from the day the Wheeler family had moved into Manor House.

Trixie didn't know what Reddy thought about all the mysteries she and Honey had solved since then. It was likely he didn't know that the two girls had been so successful that they planned to open an office when they left school and call it the Belden-Wheeler Detective Agency.

One of the girls' first cases had been to find Jim Frayne, who had run away to upstate New York to escape from his cruel stepfather. Soon afterward, Honey's parents had adopted Jim.

Jim, Trixie, and Honey, together with Brian and Mart, had formed a club called the Bob-Whites of the Glen, or B.W.G.'s for short. Another neighbor, Di Lynch, and Dan Mangan, the nephew of Bill

Regan, the Wheelers' groom, had later become Bob-Whites, too.

The Bob-Whites devoted themselves to helping others, as well as to solving the mysteries in which Trixie was constantly getting them involved.

Except this time, Trixie thought crossly, *I'm not having much luck getting Brian and Mart involved in finding out what's happened to Reddy!*

"I've already been to Manor House," Trixie said, trying to speak quietly and reasonably. "I couldn't find Honey and Jim, but I asked Regan, and he hasn't seen Reddy at all."

Mart, eleven months older than Trixie—almost her twin—stared at her thoughtfully. "I still think you're worrying over nothing," he said flatly. "Reddy can take care of himself. He's always done it before."

Trixie leaned across the table toward him. "But this time it's different," she insisted. "This time I think something's happened to him."

"What sort of something?" Brian demanded. His dark eyes watched her steadily.

For a long moment, Trixie didn't answer. Now that she was sure they were willing to listen, she wanted to be certain she remembered everything exactly the way it had happened.

Around them, the old farmhouse, where three generations of Beldens had lived, was unusually quiet. This was because Trixie's parents, almost before the sun was up, had taken her youngest brother, six-year-old Bobby, and had gone to Albany for the day, to visit friends. They would not be back until late this evening.

Now, on this March morning, Trixie was wishing with all her heart that they hadn't gone so soon. Dad and Moms would have helped search for Reddy—and they would have done it without arguing.

"Come on, Trix," Mart said impatiently. "What d'you think has happened to that dumb dog of ours?"

Trixie sighed. "That's just it—I don't know," she confessed. "But it all began last night. It was late, and I was upstairs in my room getting ready for bed. . . ."

Her story didn't take long to tell. But while she spoke, remembering what she had seen, her large blue eyes were troubled.

Some small sound from outside had drawn her to the bedroom window. She'd been just in time to see the dog's long, graceful body disappearing silently around the corner of the house.

Something about him had made her heart skip a beat. He'd looked oddly alert and intent. It was almost as if he'd just received an urgent summons, one that he could neither ignore nor resist.

At first Trixie thought the dog had spotted an intruder. She had even strained her ears to listen for Reddy's warning bark. But there had been nothing, not even the sound of his movements as he made his way to some mysterious canine destination of his own.

"So I didn't think any more about it," she finished. "But don't you see? Wherever it was he went, he didn't come back. And I've got this funny idea that keeps going around and around in my head—"

She stopped and shot an apprehensive look at Mart. She realized she had just given him another chance to tease her. Teasing Trixie was one of Mart's favorite occupations.

She waited for him to say something typical, like "The peculiar idea circulates through your peculiar cranium because there's nothing inside to stop it."

But Mart, who loved to use big words but could never spell them, said nothing. He merely continued to poke at his scrambled eggs.

Trixie was so surprised by his silence that she completely forgot what she was going to tell them next.

It was Brian who prompted her. "What funny idea keeps going around in your head?" he asked.

Trixie hesitated, then said in a rush, "I keep

thinking that maybe Reddy's hurt. Or maybe he's shut up somewhere accidentally, and he can't get out."

Puzzled, she stole another look at Mart. She was no longer sure he was even listening.

Seventeen-year-old Brian rose from the table and took his empty plate to the sink. "I still think you're worrying about nothing, Trix," he told her over his shoulder. "Reddy probably spotted a rabbit last night—or maybe it was a squirrel. Dumb dog! He ought to have learned by now that he won't catch any of 'em. They're always too quick for him."

"But supposing I'm right and you're wrong, what then?" Trixie retorted.

Brian had begun washing his dishes, but now he sighed, reached for a kitchen towel, and began wiping his hands. "Okay, Trix," he said quietly. "What d'you want us to do?"

"I want you to come and help me look for him." Trixie tried to keep the note of triumph out of her voice. She had won! Soon, with a little luck, Reddy would be found!

"I've only got one more question," Brian said. "What are you going to do about the others?"

"Others?"

"The other Bob-Whites," Brian explained patiently. "They'll be here soon to take us to school.

We volunteered to work on the grounds this morning as part of the cleanup crew, remember?"

Trixie clutched her blond curls with both hands. "Gleeps!" she exclaimed. "I forgot!"

Mart looked up suddenly and grinned. "See, Trix?" he said, the teasing note back in his voice. "I'm not the only one with a bad memory today."

"Of course," Brian added, "*most* of the Bob-Whites didn't exactly volunteer their services. *One* Bob-White volunteered for all of us. She told us *everyone* at school was going to help."

"But that's right," Trixie said breathlessly. "The custodian's sick, you see, and what with the spring dance coming up next week, there's a lot to do. So when Mr. Stratton asked for volunteers to help clean up the school—"

Mart grunted. "We know, Trix. You're the one who volunteered us."

Trixie nodded. "Except now, I don't want to go anywhere till we've found Reddy. Oh, jeepers! What am I going to do?"

Brian had turned back to the sink and was washing his dishes again. "You could answer that," he suggested as the telephone rang.

Trixie leaped out of her chair and ran to take the call. When she turned away from the phone a moment later, her eyes were sparkling.

"It's okay," she sang out. "That was Miss

Trask, and guess what!" Her happy smile widened as she thought of Honey's kind former governess, who helped run the Wheelers' estate.

"She's found Reddy?" Brian asked, smiling at his sister's enthusiasm.

"Well, Miss Trask didn't exactly find Reddy," Trixie answered excitedly, "but she *was* talking to Mr. Lytell. And he *thinks* he saw our dog not ten minutes ago."

"Aha!" Mart said softly. "So the case is closed."

"You were right, Mart," Trixie said. "He's in the woods—that is, Reddy's in the woods—at least, that's where Mr. Lytell thinks he saw him."

"There's more," Brian said. "I can feel it in my bones."

"So can we go get him in your jalopy, Brian?" Trixie asked. "I know exactly where to look, honestly! It's about a mile from Mr. Lytell's general store, and just off Glen Road—though why Reddy went there and what he's up to, I'll never know. Okay, Brian?"

Without waiting for his answer, she raced into the living room and grabbed her red Bob-White jacket from the couch, where she had thrown it only minutes before.

Her heart was singing as she shrugged herself into it, and she smiled, thinking of clever Honey, who had made matching jackets for all seven Bob-

21

Whites. Neatly cross-stitched across the backs of each one were the letters *B. W. G.*

When she ran back into the kitchen, she was glad to see Brian reaching for his Bob-White jacket, too.

He grinned at her. "I guess I'll have to take you, Trix," he said. "I'll never hear the last of it if I don't."

Trixie laughed happily. "Listen, Mart," she said, as they turned to leave, "if the others arrive before we get back—"

Mart chuckled. "Sure, I'll explain what's happened. I'll tell them you've gone to solve the mystery of the missing dog." He rose from the table and hurried away to finish his morning chores.

Trixie paused and stared down at Mart's untouched breakfast. "And when we get back, Brian," she said, "I'll solve that other mystery, too."

"What other mystery?" Brian asked, reaching into the pocket of his jeans for his car keys.

"The mystery of the ever-starving Belden," Trixie said slowly, "except Mart doesn't seem to be starving anymore. You know, Brian, I don't think Mart's been eating much for the last few days. D'you think he's worrying about something?"

Brian shook his head. "No, I don't think Mart's worried about a thing."

But as Trixie climbed into the front seat of Brian's jalopy, she was suddenly sure he was wrong.

A few minutes later, Trixie had pushed all thoughts of Mart to the back of her mind as Brian drove east along Glen Road. Soon, at Trixie's insistence, the car was slowed to a snail's pace.

"We're nearly there, Brian," Trixie warned, her keen eyes trying to watch both sides of the road at once.

Brian grunted. "We might be there, Trix, but don't expect Reddy to come running to meet us. He could be miles away by now."

"He *is* there, Brian!" Trixie cried excitedly as she caught sight of a sudden flash of bright color through the trees. She caught at her brother's arm. "It's Reddy! I'm sure of it! This is exactly the place Mr. Lytell described to Miss Trask. Oh, stop, Brian, stop!"

"Hey, watch out, Trix!" Brian exclaimed, pulling to the side of the road. "Hasn't anyone ever told you not to grab someone who's trying to drive? You could have had us both in the ditch!"

Trixie wasn't listening. Already she had jumped out of the car and was running toward the woods.

"Reddy?" she called. "Reddy, you bad dog! Where have you been? I've been so worried about you—"

The words died in her throat.

"Did you find him?" Brian asked, as he raced to join her.

Trixie pointed.

Above their heads, tall branches, not yet in bud, raised long, bare arms to the sky. Ahead, the early morning sunshine splashed dappled patterns of light across the fragrant trail that led deeper into the forest.

But Trixie had eyes only for the low bush directly ahead of her. She saw only the bright spot of color that she, and Mr. Lytell before her, had mistaken for the Beldens' Irish setter.

"What is it?" Brian asked.

Trixie ran forward and plucked the red scrap of material from its resting place. Now that she had it in her hand, she could tell that this wasn't anything like the color of Reddy's golden chestnut coat.

What she had seen had been an optical illusion—a trick that the golden sunlight had played on her eyes, and on Mr. Lytell's, too.

Brian frowned. "You know, Trix, that piece of material looks just as if it came from a man's red flannel shirt."

Wordlessly, Trixie nodded her agreement.

"But what does it mean?" Brian asked.

All at once, Trixie had to blink back the hot tears that threatened to roll down her cheeks. "It means," she said, choking back a sob, "that we haven't found Reddy, after all. Oh, Brian, where can he be?"

Worries for Trixie • 2

TEN MINUTES LATER, even Trixie had to admit that it was useless to search any farther.

Ahead, the woods stretched dense and still, while the trail they had been following ended suddenly in a dark tangle of underbrush.

"It's no good, Brian," Trixie said hopelessly. "Reddy could be anywhere."

Brian, who had come this far only at her insistence, ran his hand through his dark, wavy hair and frowned. "You know, Trix," he said, "I've been thinking. We're going at this all wrong. What we need is a search party and horses—"

"—and Bob-Whites!" Trixie exclaimed.

"Oh, Brian, you're right! D'you think that the others would come and help?" she added.

Brian grinned at her. "You know they will. I still think you're worrying about nothing, but I can see none of us are going to get any peace till we find that dog."

He turned and began leading the way back along the trail.

Trixie hurried to catch up with him. "But what about the work we're supposed to do at school? Everyone knows the Bob-Whites volunteered—"

Brian chuckled. "I doubt we'll get yelled at if we're late. More likely, no one will notice our absence at all. We're just going to have to put first things first this morning. So first, we'll find Reddy. Then, if there's time, we'll drive to school to help out."

"Great!" Trixie breathed, her eyes shining. "We'll go home now. And if the Bob-Whites aren't there—"

"We'll call them and tell them to meet us at the Wheelers' stable," Brian finished for her. "We'll explain everything to Regan. He'll be glad we're going to exercise the horses. Then we'll form a posse and search for Reddy till we find him. How's that, podner?"

He needn't have asked. A moment later, his sister, her blond curls bouncing with excitement, had raced past him to the car.

By the time he reached the car, she was already seated inside it, waiting impatiently.

She watched him put the key in the ignition and sighed happily. "Now all we need to do," she remarked, "is to find out what's wrong with Mart."

Brian didn't answer until they were well on their way home. Trixie guessed that he was wondering if Mart was sick.

Brian was constantly concerned with the well-being of everyone. The Bob-Whites knew that one day, when Jim Frayne, who had inherited a fortune, opened his school for homeless boys, Brian hoped to become its doctor.

"I think," Brian said at last, "the only thing wrong with Mart is that he's tired. He's got a history test coming up at school, he's worried about that journalism class he's taking this semester, and he was out late last night."

Trixie was surprised. "He was? Where did he go?"

Brian shrugged. "I didn't ask. Maybe he went to visit Di, or maybe he wanted to study with Jim."

Trixie sat quietly, thinking over what Brian had told her. She was also pondering Mart's recent behavior.

She frowned as she remembered how absent-minded he'd been lately. He forgot to pass on even the simplest of messages. Often he seemed to be lost in thoughts of his own. Strangest of all, he'd lost his appetite.

It was this that worried Trixie most of all. Mart had never before lost his appetite over anything. He was *always* hungry—or had been until a few days ago.

"You know what, Brian?" Trixie said at last. She stared with unseeing eyes at the familiar landscape flying past them. "I think Mart's got something on his mind—something that's worrying him a lot. He's been so moody lately. And, Brian, he hasn't even teased me!"

Brian grinned and steered the jalopy expertly into the Beldens' driveway. "If it's teasing you're missing—" he began.

Suddenly Trixie was clutching at his arm again. "They're here!" she cried, pointing at the shiny station wagon parked outside their front door. "The Bob-Whites are here! Quick! Let's hurry!"

"For crying out loud!" Brian exclaimed, slamming on the brakes. "Quit grabbing the driver!"

But his sister was already out of her seat and racing to join their friends, who were smiling and waving at them through the big car's windows.

Usually the mere sight of the station wagon was enough to make Trixie glow with pride. This was because she owned exactly a one-seventh share of it. When Mr. Wheeler had bought himself a new car, he had given the station wagon to Trixie and her friends. Now, on one door panel, neat red letters spelled out BOB-WHITES OF THE GLEN. The Bob-Whites were almost as proud of their car as they were of their club.

This morning, however, Trixie spared it barely a glance as she smiled back at its four occupants.

The car's driver, Jim Frayne, stuck his red head out of the open window. "Hey, where were you?" he asked, grinning up at her. "We thought you'd got lost. We've been waiting here for hours."

Honey Wheeler, seated beside him, laughed and tossed back her long golden hair. "Don't listen to him, Trix," she said, her wide hazel eyes twinkling. "We've only just got here, and Jim only honked twice. Are you all set to go?"

Seated behind them, Di and Dan leaned forward eagerly.

"Yes, hurry up, Trixie," Di urged. "We've got a surprise for you, and we can't wait for you to see it."

"Not only that." Dan Mangan added, grinning. "We had to drive miles this morning to get it."

"And we didn't even open it," Jim said, "so the honors are all yours, Trix."

Trixie stared at them, puzzled. They had all

been talking so fast that she hadn't had a chance to ask any of them if they'd seen the missing dog. Besides, she hadn't the slightest clue to what they were all talking about.

She could tell, though, that they were feeling pleased with themselves about something. They were gazing at her expectantly, as if they were waiting for her to break suddenly into a song of joy.

"The only surprise Trixie needs right now," Brian announced, joining her at the side of the car, "is for someone to find Reddy. He's missing, and Miss Worrywart here thinks something's happened to him."

Honey looked instantly concerned. "I'll help you search, Trix," she offered at once.

Jim was frowning. "That's strange," he said deliberately. "I wasn't able to find Patch this morning, either."

Di chuckled. "That's because both dogs are over at my place."

Trixie could hardly believe her ears. She stared and couldn't think of a thing to say.

Di looked as if she knew that she had truly astonished and pleased her friend with her news. She chuckled again at the expression on Trixie's face.

Trixie found her voice at last. "Is that the sur-

31

prise?" she asked, recovering from her amazement.

"No," Di said, shaking her head, and her long blue black hair swung gently as it framed her pretty face. "No, Trix, that's not the surprise. We didn't even know you were missing a dog."

"But I am—I mean, I was—I mean, oh, Di! Are you sure Reddy's over at your place?" Trixie felt so relieved, her tongue wouldn't work properly.

Brian chuckled. "She's trying to tell you she thought she'd nosed out another mystery," he said. "Let's see, we could have called it the secret of the Irish setter—"

"—and Jim's playful spaniel pup," Honey finished, smiling at him.

Trixie didn't mind that they were teasing her. The hard knot of worry, which had seemed to lie like a rock in the pit of her stomach, disappeared as if by magic.

"Do you feel better now?" Brian asked.

Trixie's eyes sparkled. "Oh, boy! Do I!"

So Reddy wasn't missing after all. He had just been playing with Jim's puppy, Patch, at the Lynches' big house, which stood on the highest hill beside the river. It was true that Trixie hadn't searched the Lynch grounds. She hadn't had enough time.

She couldn't help wondering what Mart was going to say when he heard the news. Probably he'd say, "I told you so." Not that she was going to worry about it. She had already done enough worrying for one day!

All at once, the whole world seemed brighter. She became aware of the soft sounds around her. It was almost as if, until this moment, she had been deaf.

She could hear the smooth purring of the car's powerful engine as it idled patiently beneath the sleek hood. She could hear the birds singing and leaves rustling as a cool breeze played tag in the old crab apple trees. It was sure going to be a beautiful day. The Bob-Whites wouldn't have to form a posse, and they could help out at Sleepyside's junior-senior high school after all.

"I'm glad that I was wrong," Trixie told Brian happily.

"To tell you the truth, I am, too, Trix," he answered. "I don't want to lose that rascal of ours any more than you do."

Honey leaned across her brother and gazed up through the car window at Trixie. "I guess you were really worried about Reddy," she said.

"I sure was," Trixie answered. "You see, he was acting so funny last night."

"Did it seem as if he'd heard someone—or something—calling him?" Jim asked suddenly.

Trixie felt a shock of surprise. "That's exactly

how he looked, Jim. How did you know?"

Jim stared at the backs of his freckled hands as they rested easily on the steering wheel. "Because that's the way I saw Patch acting last night, too. I didn't think anything of it at the time."

All at once, Trixie's fears returned in a rush. Who—or what—had attracted the dogs' attention? Had there been an intruder there, after all? Or had it been something else?

Excitement at School · 3

IN THE NEXT INSTANT, Trixie could tell that Brian was now feeling as uneasy as she was.

"Listen, Trix," he said awkwardly, "you may have been wrong about Reddy's disappearance, but maybe you were right when you thought he'd spotted something last night. I guess I'd better check around before we leave."

"I'll help, Brian," Jim offered quickly. "I don't like the sound of this any more than you do."

Dan grunted. "Let's all go."

"Yes, let's," Honey agreed quickly, clambering out of the car.

"And we'll leave Trixie's surprise till we get

back," Di added, her violet eyes sparkling.

But Trixie was no longer even thinking about surprises. She was already off and running toward that corner of the house where she had last seen their Irish setter.

When Honey caught up with her, Trixie was standing by the picnic table, staring up the hill toward the Lynch mansion.

"Did you find something?" Honey asked.

Trixie shook her head. "Not yet, Honey," she answered.

She was still puzzled fifteen minutes later, when the six Bob-Whites met once more in the cozy living room of the old farmhouse.

"No clues, no nothing," Trixie announced.

"We didn't find much, either," Brian confessed.

"Only an old cardboard carton," Jim added, "and that didn't tell us anything. It was lying by the side of the road. It fell off someone's truck, I guess. I'll clear it away later." The Bob-Whites stared at each other.

"In any case," Brian said at last, "I'm going to make sure everything's locked up tight here while we're away."

"Including the chickens?" Di asked, quickly smothering a grin.

Trixie frowned. "Chickens?"

"Di means that Mart forgot and left the gate to

the chicken run open," Jim explained.

"He's almost rounded them up," Dan said, "but I guess it's going to take him a while longer to get all of them. You want me to help you get everything locked up here, Brian?"

Brian sighed. "No, thanks, I'll do it. But I'd better give Mart a hand. For crying out loud, how could he have been dumb enough to let those chickens out?"

"See what I mean, Brian?" Trixie said slowly. "Mart's so busy worrying about something that he's just not paying attention to anything."

Brian moved toward the front door. "Why don't you guys go on to school? Mart and I will follow as soon as we can."

"But don't you want to see Trixie's surprise?" Di called after him.

Brian paused, then groaned and ran his hand through his dark, wavy hair. "Don't talk to me about surprises," he said. "I've had enough surprises this morning to last me a lifetime."

No one said anything until Jim had backed the big station wagon out of the driveway and had headed its nose in the direction of Sleepyside's junior-senior high school.

Then Honey said softly to Trixie, who was sitting beside her, "Is something wrong with Mart? What is it he's worrying about?"

"I don't know," Trixie whispered back. "But you can count on one thing, Honey. I'm going to do my best to find out—and soon!"

While the car purred quietly along the road to Sleepyside, Trixie told the remaining Bob-Whites all about her unsuccessful search that morning for Reddy.

When she had come to the end of her story, Di said suddenly, "Oh, Trix, please stop talking about missing pets. Let's talk about what we've got for you, instead. I can't wait any longer!"

Trixie turned in her seat and smiled at her friend Di. "I'm sorry, Di," she said. "I guess I almost forgot about that. What is the surprise?"

Di bent down and picked up something from the floor. The long curtain of dark hair that framed her lovely face swung forward, then was tossed back out of the way as she held whatever it was behind her back. "Here it is," she sang out. "Ta-dah!" And in the next moment, she was handing Trixie a small, neatly folded newspaper.

Trixie's cheeks flamed with excitement as she took it. "Jeepers!" she exclaimed. "Where in the world did you manage to find it? I'd never have believed it'd be so hard to find a copy of a dumb old school newspaper. But they were all gone when I tried to get one yesterday. And even Mart forgot to bring one home. The *Campus Clarion* sure is popular lately. Is the article Mart wrote for his journalism class in there? Have you read it? Is it good? Which one of our mysteries did he write about?"

Her friends laughed as Trixie finally ran out of breath. She could tell, though, that they were feeling as pleased as she was.

They all knew that Mart was taking a semester of journalism. They also knew he had been strangely silent about his new experiences as a student reporter for the school newspaper. But he *had* told them how hard he'd worked on an article for this week's issue.

"Wait till you read it," he'd told the Bob-Whites the previous week. "I wrote about all of us. We're all there."

Trixie had frowned. "I'm not sure that's a good idea," she'd said. "We don't want everyone to know about the Bob-Whites. What are you writing about? One of our mysteries?"

"Wait and you will see," Mart had answered mysteriously.

Honey's voice broke into Trixie's thoughts. "We borrowed the newspaper from a girl in one of Di's classes," she was saying eagerly. "We phoned everyone we could think of, first thing early this morning. We were lucky to find one."

"You see," Dan put in, "we knew how disappointed you were when you couldn't get a copy."

"Then we all drove for miles to pick it up," Honey said.

Trixie smiled. "So that's why you and Jim weren't at home when I came over this morning."

"You're right," Honey said, smiling. "And we don't know which mystery Mart wrote about, because we didn't look."

"We thought you'd like to do it yourself," Di said. "Oh, please open it, Trix. I'm simply dying to see. Maybe Mart's article made the front page. Wouldn't that be neat?"

There was silence as Trixie slowly unfolded the newspaper. Honey leaned close to her side, and Di and Dan crowded close to look over her shoulder.

It took only a second to see that Mart's article had not made the front page—nor the second or third. Slowly at first, then faster and faster, Trixie turned to the fourth, fifth, and sixth (and last) page.

When she had finished, she and Honey stared at each other in disappointment. Mart's article wasn't there.

"Well?" Jim demanded. "Why the dead silence? Which mystery *did* Mart write about?"

"We still don't know," Trixie said slowly. "They didn't publish it."

Honey squeezed her arm. "Never mind, Trix," she said as her brother drove into the school parking lot. "Maybe they simply didn't have room for it this week."

"And maybe," Di said suddenly, "that's what's been bothering Mart all along. Perhaps he's as disappointed as we are."

They had climbed out of the station wagon and were still standing by its side when Brian's familiar jalopy suddenly appeared. It swung into the parking space beside them.

"Boy, that was fast," Dan said admiringly. "Did you catch all the chickens?"

"Of course," Mart said, frowning. "I'd already caught 'em when Brian came to help me. You should've waited. I've just finished telling Brian so."

Brian chuckled. "I've had a lecture about it all the way here." He glanced quickly at the newspaper in Trixie's hand. "Hey, was that the surprise? Is your article there, Mart?"

"No," Mart answered hurriedly. "The journalism teacher turned it down flat."

"You could've at least told us, Mart," Trixie said reproachfully.

Mart was suddenly on the defensive. "For crying out loud!" he exclaimed. "How was I supposed to know you'd make such a big fuss over a dumb school assignment? It's no big deal, I tell you. Mr. Zimmerman just didn't like it. That's all! Forget that I even mentioned it."

Tactfully, Jim tried to change the subject. He nodded toward the cars that were crowded around them. "It sure looks like a lot of kids showed up this morning," he said.

Dan grinned. "Maybe someone," he nodded toward Trixie, "didn't have to volunteer our services today, after all."

Trixie didn't answer until the Bob-Whites were halfway across the lunch court. "There may be a lot of volunteers," she said, "but no one seems to be volunteering much energy." She pointed at the overflowing trash cans. "I wonder why someone hasn't thought of emptying those. Where is everyone, anyway?"

Puzzled, the Bob-Whites stared around them. The day before, many students had taken advantage of the unseasonably warm weather to eat outdoors, and the lunch court was still littered with the debris of the previous day's lunch period. The court was deserted, however; no one seemed interested in cleaning up the area.

Suddenly, Honey gripped Trixie's arm. "I think something's going on in front of the administration office," she exclaimed.

"You're right," Jim answered, breaking into a

run. "Come on, you guys! Maybe the office is passing out free doughnuts or something."

But in another moment, when the Bob-Whites turned the corner, they found that Jim couldn't have been more wrong.

A crowd of excited students was gathered in front of the school's office. Outside the door, Mr. Stratton, the principal, appeared to be deep in conversation with two of his teachers, who suddenly turned and hurried away.

"What is it?" Honey asked. "What's going on?"

Trixie stared at the broken window that gaped blackly against the school's dim interior. "I think someone's thrown a baseball—" she began.

But Brian was shaking his head. "It's more than a broken window, Trixie," he said, pointing. "Take a look at that!"

Trixie gasped as she gazed at the face of the building. Scrawled across it, in huge spray-painted black letters, were the words:

THE MIDNIGHT MARAUDER WAS HERE!

She heard one of the students say, "And that's not all! Mr. Stratton says this Midnight Marauder broke into the office and stole a load of cash!"

"But who *is* the Midnight Marauder?" someone else asked.

A sudden movement beside her made Trixie

turn her head sharply. She was just in time to see Mart stiffen and stand as if frozen to the spot. He was staring up at the black painted letters—and his face was white to the lips.

Mart in Trouble · 4

BEFORE TRIXIE had time to ask Mart what was wrong, Mr. Stratton had turned to face the crowd and was holding up his hand for silence.

"Students," he began, "I know you're all just as shocked as I am by what has happened."

There was a murmur of agreement from his listeners.

"As you can see," Mr. Stratton continued, "a vandal has broken into the school." His lips tightened. "Extensive damage has been done to my office, and a sum of money has been stolen from my desk."

"How much money, Mr. Stratton?" someone

in the crowd of students called out.

The principal sighed. "As far as we can figure it at the moment," he said, "there wasn't that much money to steal. Only about ten dollars was taken, we think."

Dan thrust his hands angrily into the pockets of his jeans. "I don't care if it's ten dollars or ten thousand dollars," he said in an undertone to Trixie. "The school should send for the police at once."

"I'm sure they have," Trixie whispered back. "I'll bet they called as soon as they found out what had happened. But who could've done something like this?"

It was almost as if Mr. Stratton had heard her. "We haven't yet found out who's responsible," he said grimly, "but you can be sure there's going to be an extensive investigation. Of course, the police have been called—"

"I knew it," Trixie remarked, nodding her head in approval.

"But in the meantime," Mr. Stratton continued, "if anyone here can shed any light on what's happened, I'll be in my office."

To Trixie's astonishment, she felt Mart move from her side, as if involuntarily. He took a step forward, and half raised his hand, almost as if he were going to say something. Then, in a moment, his hand dropped to his side, and he remained silent.

Puzzled, Trixie frowned.

Mr. Stratton hesitated, half turned away, then turned back to face the students once more. "I want to thank all of you for showing up this morning," he added. "Please stay away from the area where I'm standing. The police will want to examine it. But if you still feel like continuing with the cleanup job on the rest of the grounds, your help will be appreciated."

The students watched in silence as the door of the administration building closed behind him. Then they began to wander away, talking in undertones to each other.

"So that's that," Brian said. "What a rotten thing to happen."

"But now we're here," Jim said, "what d'you say we get to work?"

Honey sighed. "You're right, Jim. How about starting on the lunch court?"

Mart stared thoughtfully toward a group of his classmates who, armed with brooms and rakes, were beginning to clear the grassy area close to the school bus stop.

"Listen," he said suddenly, "can you guys manage without me for a few minutes? I need to talk to someone over there." Without waiting for an answer, Mart hurried away.

A moment later, Trixie saw him talking earnestly to a tall, dark-haired boy who didn't seem to like what Mart was saying. Trixie saw the boy scowl and shake his head.

"Who is that?" Di said in her ear.

"I was just wondering the same thing," Trixie answered slowly, still watching the two boys.

"His name is Lester Mundy," Dan said shortly. "I think the kid's in Mart's math class."

Trixie looked at him. "It doesn't sound as if you like him much."

"He's the class clown," Brian explained. "He's also a renowned practical joker."

"Like Ben Riker?" Trixie asked, then wished she hadn't. She glanced quickly at Honey to see if she had been listening.

Honey had. She laughed and squeezed Trixie's arm. "No one's as good a practical joker as Ben Riker, Trix," she said, "though sometimes I think Lester comes pretty close."

Trixie sighed as she remembered Honey's cousin. She had never thought Ben Riker's practical jokes were funny. Ben did dumb things like putting sugar into salt shakers and salt into sugar bowls.

Once, during one of the Bob-White's early adventures, Trixie had pretended to like Ben a lot, even though everyone knew she liked Jim best.

Trixie could feel her face growing hot just thinking about it. "If Lester's jokes are anything like Ben's," she said hurriedly, "then I hope Mart knows what he's doing."

Jim chuckled as he led the way to the supply room. "I hope he does, too. If not, he's likely to find a frog in his locker—"

"Or spiders in his gym shoes," Brian added quickly, pulling open the door and ushering his friends inside.

Di gasped in horror and stared around at the room's dark shelves. If there was one thing she couldn't stand it was spiders. The Bob-Whites could still remember the time when her phony uncle had tried to frighten her with one.

"You—you don't suppose Lester will try anything like that on us, do you?" Di said at last, her voice shaking.

"We'll see that he doesn't," Brian promised, and handed her a broom.

Di looked at it carefully before she took it from him. Trixie could see that she was apprehensive.

"Maybe Lester does silly things to try and get attention," kindhearted Honey said slowly. "Maybe he's lonely."

Dan grunted. "Then I've got news for him," he said as he passed out large plastic trash bags to each of his friends. "He's making a big mistake."

"Maybe he is," Honey answered, "but—oh, don't you see? We Bob-Whites are never lonely. We've all got each other. But some of the kids at school always seem to be left out of everything. It's as if no one knows they're even alive. Take Ruthie Kettner, for instance."

Di frowned. "Who's Ruthie Kettner?"

Honey opened the supply room door wide so that the Bob-Whites had a clear view of the school's main entrance.

A stockily built, fair-haired girl was standing alone by the front steps. "That's Ruthie Kettner," Honey said.

Trixie noticed that Ruthie was staring toward the cleanup crew by the bus stop, and at Mart and Lester who were still deep in conversation. It seemed almost as if Ruthie were as interested in what Mart was talking about as Trixie herself.

"I've never seen Ruthie talk to anyone," Honey said thoughtfully. "I think the poor kid's very shy."

Honey's huge hazel eyes clouded over, and she lowered her head so that her shoulder-length honey blond hair shaded her face. Trixie guessed that her friend was remembering the days before she'd come to live in Sleepyside, when she had been sent away to boarding schools and had been lonely, too.

"I'll tell you what," Trixie said. "We'll ask Ruthie if she wants to help us in the lunch court this morning. How's that?"

Honey raised her head and smiled. "I think that would be great."

Dan grinned. "Don't worry. I'll go and ask her. Don't forget, before I joined the Bob-Whites, I knew what it was like to feel unwanted, too."

Before Dan could move, however, Trixie saw Mart suddenly leave Lester's side and come racing across the grass.

"Ruthie?" he was yelling. "Hey, Ruthie? You got a minute? I want to talk to you."

The Bob-Whites saw Ruthie's face flush scarlet. She half turned, as if she were going to hurry away. Then she seemed to change her mind, and took a step toward him instead.

In another instant, the two of them were walking toward a bench under a tall maple tree, and Mart's blond head was bent toward hers.

Trixie's blue eyes widened with surprise. "Jeepers!" she exclaimed. "Mart must have known what we were going to do."

"Or maybe," Honey replied, giggling, "Ruthie's been reading the advice to the lovelorn in the school newspaper. Last week Miss Lonelyheart told someone that to *have* a friend, you must *be* a friend."

51

"Not very original," Jim remarked as he led the way to the lunch court, "but very true."

He smiled at Trixie over his shoulder, and everyone laughed. They knew that ever since their very first adventure together, Trixie could do no wrong as far as Jim was concerned.

"It beats me why that Miss Lonelyheart column is so popular," Brian said. "Ever since it began appearing in the school newspaper several weeks ago, the kids have been doing nothing else but talk about it."

"And grabbing all the copies they can get," Trixie answered, remembering how she'd been unable to get even one copy the previous day.

She stared with unseeing eyes at an overflowing trash can.

"Does anyone know which teacher is writing it?" Honey asked.

"I think it's one of the counselors," Di said. "But I wonder which one."

"Maybe Mart could tell us," Dan suggested.

Trixie shook her head. "I don't think so. He told me once that Mr. Zimmerman, the journalism teacher, is the only one who knows for sure, and he hasn't said anything about it."

"I wonder why not." Dan asked.

Honey giggled. "Miss Lonelyheart's probably afraid she'd be swamped with letters and phone calls at her home every day."

"And her classroom would be crowded with problem kids wanting to ask her advice," Trixie agreed.

"I know what *I'd* ask Miss Lonelyheart," Brian said suddenly.

Honey's face flushed. "Do you have troubles with a lonely heart, Brian?" she asked shyly.

Brian laughed. "Not in the way you mean, Honey. I'd merely ask her what to do with a certain brother who promised to help us clean up this morning, but who isn't here. Where is Mart, anyway?"

Mart was still missing an hour later, when the rest of the Bob-Whites looked with satisfaction at the results of their handiwork.

They had worked hard. They were hot and tired, but the lunch court and its surrounding area were swept and free of debris.

"Okay," Brian said at last. "I guess we're all through here. Where to now?"

Di laughed and pushed her long hair back from her pretty, flushed face. "I vote we take a rest," she answered promptly.

"Me, too," Honey said.

Jim chuckled. "Me, three."

Honey looked at Trixie who seemed to be deep in thought. "How about it, Trix?" Honey said.

"Do you want to take a break?"

"What I really want," Trixie replied slowly, "is the answers to three questions." She ticked them off on her fingers. "One: What did Reddy and Patch see last night? Two: Which teacher is Miss Lonelyheart?"

"And three?" Di asked, as Trixie hesitated.

"And three:" Trixie said thoughtfully, "Who is the Midnight Marauder?"

"Number three's easy," a voice said in her ear. Trixie turned sharply and found herself staring into the grinning face of Lester Mundy.

"Well?" Honey demanded. "Who *is* the Midnight Marauder?"

Lester sniggered. "The police arrested him not half an hour ago," he said. "The Midnight Marauder is none other than Mart Belden!"

More Worries • 5

FOR A MOMENT, Trixie was so shocked that she couldn't even move.

"I'll bet that surprised you," Lester said, "but it's all true, every word."

Trixie found her voice at last. "But it isn't true!" she exclaimed hotly. "It can't be! I don't believe it! You've made a mistake!"

"Or else he's trying to pull one of his practical jokes on us," Brian said, clenching his fists.

"Yeah," Jim agreed, "a very bad practical joke."

"Hey, back off!" Lester cried in alarm as he stared at the circle of angry Bob-White faces. "It's not my fault. I only came to give you the news, that's all. Don't get mad at me! Get mad at Sergeant Molinson. He's the one who did the arresting. He's taken Mart downtown for questioning. I just thought you ought to know."

There was a stunned silence as the Bob-Whites stared at each other.

To Trixie, it was as if she was in the middle of a bad dream. "Is this true?" she asked Lester, her voice low. But she sensed what his answer was going to be even before he nodded his head.

"Oh, Brian!" Di cried, clutching his arm. "What are we going to do?"

Trixie swallowed hard. "There's no need for anyone else to worry about this," she said. "Brian's car is here, and he and I will just go and see what this is all about. The rest of you can go on home. . . ."

But already the Bob-Whites were shaking their heads.

"No, we'll come with you, Trix," Honey said, moving quickly to her friend's side.

"That's right," Dan put in. "There's been some mistake made, that's all."

"We'll all go," Di announced.

"I agree," Jim said quietly.

"Well, now, and isn't that just great!" Lester exclaimed, staring at them. "All for one and one for all"— he sniggered—"even if one is a crook!"

He took to his heels and raced away before anyone could answer him.

"O-o-h! That boy!" Trixie stormed, her blue eyes flashing.

"Ignore him, Trix!" Brian answered sharply. "We've got more important things to think about for now."

"Lucky for Lester!" Trixie retorted.

Even as she spoke, she realized that it was easier to feel angry at Lester than worried about Mart's arrest.

She didn't even have to wonder if Mart was guilty of having vandalized the school. She knew without any question that he hadn't done it. Sergeant Molinson should have known it, too. Obviously he didn't, because otherwise he wouldn't have taken Mart away as if he were some sort of common criminal.

All the same, her thoughts were in a turmoil as she, Honey, and Di made their way back to the parking lot, while the boys hurried to put away all the cleaning equipment.

"And Brian's also going to check with Mr. Stratton," Trixie told the two girls, "just in case Lester was merely playing a joke."

But when Brian joined her five minutes later, she could tell from his face that most of the news

Lester had brought them was all too true.

"Mart *has* been taken downtown for questioning," Brian was quick to tell them, "but then so have several other students. Mart hasn't been arrested, though, so you can relax a little, Trix."

"But why do they want to question him?" Trixie cried. "He doesn't know anything about this."

Brian didn't quite look at her, and he seemed to be trying to think how to frame his answer. "It seems that someone saw him on the school grounds last night," he said finally and rather hesitantly.

"But that can't be right," Trixie exclaimed. "Mart was over at Di's."

Di stared. "At my house?"

"Well, wasn't he?" Trixie asked, bewildered.

"No," Di answered. "I was home all evening."

"Then he was with Jim—" Trixie stopped as Jim shook his head.

"He wasn't with me, either," he said awkwardly.

"Then where was he?" Trixie demanded.

"Come on, Trix," Honey said, opening the passenger door of the station wagon. "Climb in and let's go. We can figure it all out later."

In the end, Trixie decided to ride in her brother's jalopy, while the Bob-Whites' big car followed them all the way into town.

As Brian pulled up outside the police station, he

said suddenly, "I'm afraid there's something I haven't told you, Trix. The school wasn't the only place that was robbed and vandalized last night. Wimpy's was, too."

Speechless, Trixie stared at him as she thought of one of their favorite eating places—the hamburger parlor that looked like a train's dining car.

"Whoever it was," Brian was saying, "broke in late last night. He stole over a hundred dollars in cash and—are you ready for this?—a whole load of hamburger patties from Wimpy's freezer."

"Hamburger patties?" Trixie slowly echoed in astonishment.

Brian nodded. "And here's something that's really weird. The Midnight Marauder wrote letters both to the school and to Wimpy's. For some reason, the post office didn't deliver them till today. But, Trixie, the Marauder's letters were warnings. He told them beforehand what he was going to do!"

Trixie was still thinking about these strange events as she and her friends raced into the police station.

They saw Mart at once. He was sitting dejectedly on a bench against the far wall. Three other boys, none of whom Trixie recognized, were sitting with him.

Mart jumped to his feet as soon as he saw the Bob-Whites. "You shouldn't have come," he exclaimed, hurrying toward them. "There's nothing you can do. Didn't Ruthie give you my message?"

"We haven't seen Ruthie since you were talking to her a while ago," Trixie said. "Oh, Mart, are you okay? What's this all about?"

Before he could answer, a door opened on the far side of the room, and Sergeant Molinson was beckoning to Mart to follow him.

Mart hesitated, then swung on his heel and moved away. "I'll explain later," he said over his shoulder. "Don't go away. I'll be through with this in a minute."

Trixie was scarcely comforted when, a second later, Sergeant Molinson's office door banged shut behind him. Somehow, it sounded final, as if they would never see Mart again.

"Maybe we ought to call Dad and Moms," Trixie said, on the point of tears. "If Mart's in trouble, they'd want to know about it."

Brian had obviously been thinking the same thing, because he answered at once, "Let's hold off for a while, Trix. Maybe Mart is right, and he'll be through in a few minutes."

All the same, it was another long, interminable thirty minutes before the door opened once more and Mart came hurrying toward them. He was followed by Sergeant Molinson's heavy figure.

"So," Sergeant Molinson said, when he saw Trixie, "I might have known that Miss Detective Belden would be here."

"But why would you want to question my brother?" Trixie cried hotly. "He doesn't know anything about what happened at school—or at Wimpy's, either."

"Ah, so you heard about Wimpy's?" Sergeant Molinson looked at her thoughtfully.

"She knows only what I've just told her," Brian put in, "and I know only what the school principal told me."

Dan frowned. "We've just heard about it," he said, "and it doesn't make sense."

"Not unless a teen-ager's behind all this," Sergeant Molinson replied, staring hard at Mart. "We don't yet have any evidence to arrest anyone, but we're going to get it. You can count on it."

For the second time that morning, Trixie thought her almost-twin was on the point of volunteering some sort of information. Exactly what it was, she couldn't imagine.

In the next moment, however, it was obvious that Mart had changed his mind, because all he said was, "Is it okay, then? Can I go?"

"You can go for now," Sergeant Molinson answered, turning away, "but don't go far. I'll have some questions to ask you later."

The Bob-Whites were silent until they were standing on the sidewalk once more.

Then Trixie burst out, "All right, Mart. Now tell us. What's going on? What's worrying you? How could Sergeant Molinson even begin to suspect you of being the Midnight Marauder? Were you on the school grounds last night? Oh, Mart, what is it you know that you're not telling anyone —even us?"

Mart was silent for a long moment. Then he raised his head and looked into her worried blue eyes. "All right, Trix," he said at last. "I guess I'd better tell you. But I warn you, you're not going to like it. Let's go on home, and then—"

He never completed his sentence. His gaze sharpened suddenly as he stared at something over Trixie's left shoulder.

She swung around to see what had caught his attention.

At first, she could see nothing unusual. The usual number of Saturday morning shoppers seemed to be hurrying along the street. Then she noticed that they all seemed to be hurrying in one direction. Their steps slowed as they neared Crimper's department store. It was an old two-story building that had been there as long as Trixie could remember.

"What is it?" Honey asked, turning her head to see what Mart and Trixie were looking at.

Trixie frowned. "Everyone seems to be watching something on top of Crimper's roof. Come on; let's go and look."

The Bob-Whites raced along the sidewalk and joined others whose necks were craning upward.

Trixie saw the store's upper story, where shoppers and salespeople alike were crowded at the windows, trying to peer upward. Her sharp eyes scanned the roof's eaves. "I can't see anything," she said at last.

"Me, either," Honey said, pressing close to her friend.

All along, Mart had been busy scanning the crowd. "I think you'll find the only thing your orbs can discern," he announced, with a sudden return to his old manner, "is a certain person playing one of his excruciating jokes. It's the most ancient trick in the lexicon."

"What's a lexicon?" Di whispered.

"The theory," Mart went on, "is that if you stare at something long enough and hard enough, others will naturally think there is something to stare at. Thus a joke has been accomplished."

"I don't understand," Honey said, bewildered.

Mart put his hand on her shoulder and pointed at Crimper's roof. "There," he said, "is the star*ee*.

And there," he swung his arm, "is the star*er*."

The Bob-Whites saw someone standing on the sidewalk's edge, convulsed with laughter.

Suddenly Trixie's eyes widened as she noticed his bicycle parked at the curb behind him. Strapped to its rear rack was a can of black spray paint, obviously just purchased.

"And that," said Mart, "is who *I* think is causing all the trouble. That, Trix, is the Midnight Marauder."

And he pointed straight at Lester Mundy!

Inside Crimper's • 6

MART'S ANNOUNCEMENT took Trixie completely by surprise. She wasn't sure exactly what it was she'd expected him to tell her, but it certainly wasn't this.

Brian obviously hadn't been expecting this, either. He frowned at his brother. "Are you sure about that statement you've just made, Mart?" he asked sharply. "That's a serious accusation."

"And if it's true," Dan said, "you ought to turn right around and march back to the police station. Sergeant Molinson will want to know everything about it."

"Of course I'm not sure," Mart retorted. His

arm dropped slowly to his side. "If I was sure, don't you think I'd have told someone about it before now? The thing is, you see, I can't prove anything. As I told you, *I* think it's Lester. On the other hand, it could just as well be Shrimpy Davis —or Marvin Easton—or Ruthie Kettner— or—"

Trixie gasped. "Ruthie Kettner? But that's impossible!"

"The whole thing's impossible, Trix," Mart answered. He watched as Lester, still grinning, suddenly jumped on his bike and sped away.

Honey looked as bewildered as Trixie felt. "I know Ruthie Kettner," she said, "but who are those other people you've just named? Why do you suspect them? And why are you so worried?"

"Come on, Mart," Jim said. "You can tell us. It'll make you feel better. Why did Sergeant Molinson bring you down here for questioning? Why should he think you were responsible for all this vandalism that's going on? He *can't* think you're guilty."

"I'm afraid he does," Mart replied, gazing around at the circle of concerned faces. "And what's more—" he swallowed hard—"he's right."

Afterward Trixie found that she could remember almost every detail of that morning. The sun, which had shone so brightly at the day's beginning, was now covered by gray, billowy clouds that scudded across the sky.

A sudden chill gust of wind swirled across the town square. It caused the people standing in front of Crimper's to clutch at hats and head scarves and to pull their coats tightly around them.

Already the crowd was dispersing, though several people, reluctant to believe that there was absolutely nothing to see, still turned their heads to stare upward.

It was Brian who took charge after Mart's second startling announcement. "We need to talk," he said, "privately."

"And right now," Trixie added. "Let's go to Wimpy's—"

But already Brian was shaking his head. "Wimpy's is closed for today," he said. "The vandal made a mess of the place."

"We could go home," Di suggested.

"Or we could go in here," Honey said, nodding toward Crimper's front entrance.

Trixie knew that her friend was thinking of the small, old-fashioned dining room on the second floor, which catered to many of Sleepyside's older residents.

"I vote that we go home," she said promptly. "We can cook hot dogs and make hot chocolate— and Mart can explain everything."

In the end, it was the weather that put an end to all further discussion. The sky darkened, and it began to rain, lightly at first, then harder.

The Bob-Whites hesitated no longer. They made a dive for the department store's front entrance and hurried inside.

Instantly, Trixie felt, as she always did, that she had somehow stepped into another world.

Her mother had once told her that Crimper's hadn't changed much since she herself was a little girl. Heavy wooden counters, some with glass tops, offered such things as pins and needles, embroidery silks and knitting yarns, towels and tablecloths, underclothes and nightgowns, beauty preparations and costume jewelry.

Around the store's dark-paneled walls, shelves were stacked with mysterious boxes that, when opened, were found to contain nothing more exciting than scarves or stockings, gloves or handkerchiefs.

It was here, at Crimper's, that Trixie's grandmother had searched for bargains among the many brightly colored bolts of materials. And it was here, in the clothing department, that Trixie could still remember choosing clothes for her first exciting day in kindergarten.

In spite of her eagerness to hear Mart's story, Trixie couldn't resist avoiding the wide wooden staircase at the back of the store. It led to the housewares and home furnishings departments, as well as to the restaurant, on the second floor.

Instead, she led the way to the ornate and creaking elevator beside it. Mart had once said that it wheezed like an asthmatic dowager, but Trixie had always liked it.

She was fascinated by its glass-fronted entrance doors and by its heart-stopping, jolting ride. She often thought its passengers could never be entirely certain that the elevator was going to reach its destination.

Dan obviously thought so, too. "Are you sure this thing is safe, Trix?" he asked, stepping gingerly inside it.

"Trixie likes to believe it isn't," Brian answered, "but I've never yet known it to break down."

He waited until all his friends were inside before he moved the old-fashioned lever to start their ride.

Jim looked around at the elevator's red velvet interior and polished brass handrails. "Boy," he said admiringly, "they sure knew how to build things to last in the old days. Don't you think so, Trix?"

Absently, Trixie nodded, though she wasn't really listening. She found her thoughts returning again and again to Mart's puzzling statement of a few minutes ago. What had he meant when he said that he was responsible for the actions of the Midnight Marauder? What could it be that he was going to tell them?

She glanced at his silent figure standing beside her. Then she stiffened when she found that he was staring intently at the main floor below them.

Trixie followed his gaze. She saw the rain beating against the store's large plate glass windows. She saw customers in front of counters and salespeople behind them.

She saw young Mr. Crimper, who was now the store manager, since his father had retired. He sat in his glass-fronted office just inside the main entrance. As she watched, he caught sight of her in the slowly ascending elevator, and he smiled and waved his hand.

Trixie raised her hand to wave back. But in the next instant, the smile froze on her face. Suddenly she realized what had attracted Mart's attention.

Ruthie Kettner was standing in the store's far corner, which was reserved for artists' supplies. She was about to make a purchase—and that purchase was a large paintbrush.

"Maybe," Mart said slowly, "I was wrong about Lester Mundy after all. Maybe it's Ruthie who's the Midnight Marauder."

Trixie frowned. "Whoever it is," she replied, "I

know one thing for sure. If you're that worried about it, we'd better find out—and fast."

When the elevator jolted to a stop, Trixie was the first one out of it. Quickly she led the others to the restaurant's entrance and stood looking about her.

Although it was still early for lunch, many of the tables were filled with people who were lingering over their morning coffee. Trixie guessed that they were really waiting for the rain to stop.

At a table a short distance away, two dark-haired women were deep in conversation—although the small, thin one seemed to be doing all the talking. The other, a sharp-faced woman in her early thirties, appeared to be asking occasional questions and taking notes of the answers.

Trixie stared at the notetaker. "Who is that?" she asked.

Mart scowled. "Her name's Vera Parker, and she's a reporter for the *Sleepyside Sun*. She's been snooping around all morning." He sighed. "I think she's planning to write an article about juvenile delinquents. I heard Sergeant Molinson talking to her earlier."

"And who's the other lady?" Honey asked. "I've seen her somewhere before."

"That's Margo Birch," Di answered promptly.

"She's a well-known New York antique dealer. I think she lives around here, though. She's been interviewed on television—"

"And hasn't her picture been on the cover of magazines and stuff like that?" Jim interrupted.

Di nodded.

"Maybe that reporter's planning on doing *two* articles," Dan remarked. "One on antiques and the other on—"

"Juvenile delinquency?" Margo Birch said, raising her voice suddenly. "Ah, yes, I could say a lot on that subject. It's one of the major problems of our society today." She smiled at her companion. "Though, of course, I don't pretend to be an expert on *that* matter."

The reporter leaned across the table and asked a question that Trixie couldn't hear.

Margo Birch settled back in her chair. "Why, my dear," she drawled loudly, "but I don't blame the youngsters at all. No, not in the slightest. It's *parents*, you see, who must bear the full responsibility for the actions of their children. Oh, yes, spare the rod and spoil the child. An old saying, but a true one."

Mart shifted uncomfortably from one foot to the other.

All at once, Trixie had a feeling that it had been a mistake to come here. She had been right all along, wanting to go home to talk. At home it was safe—and quiet. At Crabapple Farm there were no loud, insistent voices from which to try to escape.

"Now take the business with this disturbed teen-ager," Margo Birch was saying. "Everyone's been talking about it this morning. What is it he's calling himself? The Midnight Marauder?"

Vera Parker seemed to be about to answer. Then she turned her head and saw the Bob-Whites watching from the doorway. Then she said something in an undertone to Margo Birch.

In the next moment, there was one of those inexplicable silences in the restaurant. It was as if everyone had, for some reason, stopped talking to hear what was going to happen next.

What happened next was that Margo Birch opened her eyes wide and said, in a penetrating whisper, "One of the suspects? Where? Which one? Oh, my goodness, but you simply must point him out."

Immediately, everyone seemed to be staring in the same direction—toward the Bob-Whites.

Trixie heard one man say loudly, "Did you hear that? One of those kids is the Midnight Marauder. I'll bet it's that blond kid with the curly hair and the sulky expression, who—"

Mart didn't wait to hear any more. At once he

73

turned sharply on his heel and strode out of the restaurant. His ears were red, and Trixie could see that the back of his neck was, too.

Mart didn't wait for the creaking elevator. He rushed for the top of the wide staircase and was already halfway down it when the Bob-Whites caught up with him.

"Ooh! What an awful woman!" Trixie stormed, her blue eyes flashing with indignation. "I don't think I like that Margo Birch one little bit."

"Or Vera Parker, either," Honey said loyally as they all hurried to the store's main entrance. "I'm sorry, Mart. I shouldn't even have suggested Crimper's at all."

"Forget it, Honey," Mart answered, over his shoulder. "You couldn't have known anything like that was going to happen. And I suppose I'd better get used to being thought of as Public Enemy Number One until this business is over and done with."

Trixie didn't say anything until they were standing once more on the wet sidewalk. The rain had stopped as suddenly as it had started, though the wind was stronger than it had been before.

Trixie shivered, then burst out, "The whole thing is simply stupid!"

"I know," Mart said, thrusting his hands deep into the pockets of his jeans, "which is why I need the help of all of my friends."

"Let's go to my place," Di suggested suddenly, "and that way our cook can fix us lunch while Mart tells us everything."

Dan grunted. "And this time *nothing's* going to stop us."

So many things had happened already that Trixie wouldn't have been at all surprised if this time, too, some other form of disaster was about to prevent them from hearing what Mart had to say.

But nothing did. Half an hour later, they faced Mart in Di's sumptuous family room and settled themselves down to listen.

"It all began," Mart said, staring out of the large windows, "a few weeks ago, when I started my journalism class."

Trixie frowned. "I don't see what that's got to do with anything."

Honey put her finger to her lips. "Hush, Trix. Let's hear the rest of it."

"Yes," Brian said, nodding his dark head. "No more interruptions now."

Mart kept his gaze fixed on the wide expanse of green lawn. "You might say that 'Some people are born great, others achieve greatness, and others have greatness thrust upon them.' That's a famous quotation."

"I don't care about any dumb old quotation," Trixie cried, forgetting that she had intended to keep quiet. "Tell us what your journalism class has got to do with the Midnight Marauder."

"It's got virtually everything to do with it," Mart answered.

Di giggled. "Though, now I come to think of it, that quotation did sound as though it came straight from the school newspaper. Miss Lonely-heart is always quoting stuff like that."

Jim raised his red head sharply. "Hey, that's right!"

Trixie sighed and forgot her good intentions again. "I still can't help wondering which one of the counselors really is Miss Lonelyheart," she said thoughtfully.

Mart shoved one hand into the pocket of his jeans and nervously jingled the coins he found there. "As for that," he said, "it's the easiest question to answer out of this whole rotten mess."

Trixie stared. "It is? But I thought you didn't know. All right, then. Who *is* Miss Lonelyheart?"

Mart turned from the window at last and faced his friends. "Haven't you guessed?" he asked miserably. "Miss Lonelyheart is *me*."

Mart's Confession • 7

THERE WAS stunned silence. Then everyone began talking at once.

"You?" Trixie said. "Did you say *you* were Miss Lonelyheart?"

"If this is one of your jokes—" Brian began.

Di blushed crimson. "Oh, no! I—I just wrote a letter to Miss Lonelyheart only last week—"

"But—but you *can't* be Miss Lonelyheart, Mart!" Honey exclaimed.

"But he's not joking," Dan put in. "Look at Mart's face."

There was another silence, while Mart's face and neck turned beet red.

"Go ahead," he burst out at last. "Why don't you all laugh? I know you want to. If it were me listening, I'd be falling on the floor in hysterics by now. Didn't you get it? I'm Miss Lonelyheart. I've been Miss Lonelyheart all along. Me, Mart Belden!"

Jim's mouth was twitching, but he managed to say solemnly, "We're not laughing, Mart. Honest!"

"Of course not," Brian added, without quite looking at his brother.

"We wouldn't laugh over anything like that, would we, Trix?" Honey said, avoiding her best friend's eyes.

Trixie struggled to swallow back the laughter that she could feel beginning to bubble up from somewhere deep inside her. "No," she said, trying vainly to stop her voice from shaking. "We wouldn't laugh over anything like that, would we?" Then all at once, she started to giggle. "Well, would we?" she demanded, and her eyes began to water. Then she answered her own question. "Yes, we would!" And she threw back her head and shouted with laughter, while Mart glared across the room at her.

Trixie's laughter was contagious, and in the next moment, first Honey, and then the others began laughing with her.

Mart did his best to hang on to what dignity he could. "It's not funny," he kept repeating. "Aw, come on, you guys. It's not *that* funny."

But it *was* that funny, because Mart's news had been so unexpected. The more he protested, the more the Bob-Whites howled with laughter, until Mart himself began to smile and finally to laugh, ruefully, with the others.

They were still laughing a few minutes later, when Harrison, the Lynches' reserved and solemn butler, appeared in the doorway. He raised a disapproving eyebrow at the Bob-Whites' hilarity, which made them laugh harder than ever.

"Lunch is served, miss," Harrison announced to Di at last, when he could make himself heard.

Mart stopped laughing instantly. "Good," he said promptly. "I'm starved. Come on, everyone. Didn't you hear? It's lunchtime, and I'm about to faint if I don't get something to eat."

"Besides," Honey said, wiping her eyes, "we've still got to hear the rest of Mart's news."

"You're r-right, Honey," Trixie gasped, holding her side, which now ached from laughing so hard. "And I don't know why I should think so, but it'll even be good to see Mart's appetite back to normal at last."

She was not disappointed. For the first time in weeks, Mart ate everything that was put in front of him.

Even Harrison stood approvingly at Mart's elbow

while Trixie's almost-twin demolished three bowl-fuls of soup, half a dozen ham and cheese sand-wiches, and two huge wedges of chocolate cake.

While Harrison was in the room, the Bob-Whites talked idly among themselves of unimpor-tant matters, though Trixie could tell that every-one was thinking about what Mart would tell them as soon as lunch was over.

Mart must have known it, too, for the door had no sooner closed behind Harrison's stiff back than he leaned forward and said, "Okay, is everyone ready now?"

The Bob-Whites nodded solemnly, and sat back in their chairs to listen.

"It all began," Mart said, "as I told you, when I joined Mr. Zimmerman's journalism class. It started out fine, except I couldn't seem to write the stuff old Zimmerman wanted to print."

"What really did happen about last week's arti-cle, Mart?" Trixie asked.

Mart scowled. "It was just like I told you, Trix. It was another article I'd slaved over, and Zim-merman didn't like it."

"And did you write up one of our adventures?" Honey asked.

Mart shook his head. "No, I didn't write about one of them. I wrote about them all."

Trixie gasped. "Every one?"

"Every one," Mart replied, "and d'you know what old Zimmerman said? He said I had a good imagination, but the whole article was unbelievable. Can you beat it? Our adventures *couldn't* have happened, as far as he was concerned."

"You're getting ahead of yourself, Mart," Brian said firmly. "Tell us about—" his mouth twitched— "Miss Lonelyheart."

Mart sighed. "I really backed into that one. I kept on writing articles, like I told you. And old Zimmerman kept turning them down, so I tried to think of something he *would* accept."

"And?" Honey prompted.

"And so I got this idea of writing a regular weekly column." Mart's face was flushed again. "I didn't mean for it to get out of hand, honest! I got to thinking it could be something like household hints, or something similar."

"I think that was a good idea," Honey said at once. "Lots of people like to read stuff like that."

"I looked into that old book that Moms uses all the time," Mart confessed, looking at Trixie. "There're all kinds of things in there, like how to get stains out of tablecloths, and how to keep cut flowers from wilting—"

Trixie nodded. "I remember."

Mart bit his lip. "But then I had to get clever," he said. "Shortly after Mr. Zimmerman had approved a household hints column, I overheard a couple of the guys talking in the gym. One of them wanted to know how he should go about asking a girl to go with him to the spring dance. So I stuck that question in the column, too, along with my answer."

Brian looked at his brother. "Which was?"

"The only way to find out if a girl wants to go out with you," Mart answered promptly, "is to ask her."

Brian nodded approvingly. "That sounds fine to me."

Mart sighed. "It sounded fine to Mr. Zimmerman, too. He approved the copy—even the dumb name I thought up, which, as you now know, was 'Miss Lonelyheart.' And that was my big mistake."

"Why didn't you sign your own name, Mart?" Trixie asked.

"I didn't think anyone would want to read the stuff if they knew who was writing it," Mart said, leaning his elbows on the table. "It seemed like a good idea at the time. But then, you see, the stupid column really caught on as soon as it appeared in the paper."

Dan grunted. "So then what happened?"

"What happened was," Mart answered slowly, "the school's newspaper office was shortly flooded with heartrending missives. And it soon became clear that lots of kids wanted advice about their love life." He looked down at his hands. "At first, I could handle it. I printed their questions as well as my answers."

"I remember," Honey said, "and a lot of your answers were funny."

Mart nodded. "I know. I thought the whole thing was funny. That was then. But soon I began getting other kinds of letters. Some of the kids had *real* problems."

"What kind of problems, Mart?" Brian said.

Mart sighed again. "Some kids felt that no one liked them. They were unpopular at school—and often at home, too."

Trixie thought of her own happy home life. Instantly, she felt sympathetic toward those schoolmates who didn't know the warm feeling of being loved and wanted. "Oh, Mart, how awful!" she exclaimed, her voice trembling.

"But that wasn't all," Mart said, looking at her. "Some of these kids, Trix, have got a real raw deal out of life. One girl wrote about her father. She said he drank—a lot. I guess he was an alcoholic. She wanted to know what she should do. Another said her mother had left home a couple of months ago. She just picked up and walked out on the whole family. The father didn't know where she'd gone or why she'd left or anything. So now he's trying to raise six kids all by himself. The girl who wrote the letter wanted to know what 'Miss Lonelyheart' would advise her to do about it. How could she get her mother back?"

Di gasped. "But that's terrible, Mart! What did you tell her—and that one with the alcoholic father, too?"

"I couldn't handle it." Mart's voice was low. "How could I tell people what to do with problems like those? I told them to see their counselors. That's what I told most of them—when they'd signed their letters, that is. But a lot of them wrote in anonymously—and those letters I answered as best I could when I printed them." He raised his head and looked at his friends. "It's been just awful these last few weeks. I haven't had any idea what to do."

Brian shifted sharply in his chair. "And so we come to the Midnight Marauder business," he said. "What do you know about that?"

"It all began," Mart said miserably, "when I started to get a series of letters. Every time, they were shoved under the door of Mr. Zimmerman's office and addressed to 'Miss Lonelyheart.' Some of 'em were so bad, I never showed them to old Zimmerman at all. Whoever had written the letters hated school, hated the teachers, and ranted on about how one day he was going to do something desperate."

"How did you handle it, Mart?" Brian asked, staring at his brother.

Mart shrugged his shoulders. "I handled it as best I could. The letters weren't signed, so I didn't know who it was. At first, I kidded the writer along and made out that things weren't as bad as he—or she—thought they were. I used to leave the answers taped to the outside of old Zimmerman's office door. I had to ask his permission to do that, of course."

"But what happened then?" Trixie persisted. "You must have *some* reason for thinking this same person is the Midnight Marauder. Did you keep all his letters?"

"I didn't dare," Mart confessed. "Some of 'em were really bad, so I threw them away. I only kept the last one." He reached slowly into the back pocket of his jeans and pulled out a much-crumpled and obviously well-thumbed letter. "I got this last Thursday," he said. "Here"—he pushed it across the table to Trixie—"you read it and see what I mean."

Trixie scanned the letter quickly. Then she looked up and announced, "It's written in block capitals, and this is what it says: 'Dumb Miss Lonelyheart: You think you're so smart with your slick answers, but let me tell you something. I've tried everything, and nothing's worked. I'm fed up with being ignored by everyone at school. No matter what I do, no one likes me, so now I'm really going to do something to make people sit up and take notice. A desperate situation calls for desperate measures. I've made up my mind. Saturday's the day! You have been warned!' "

Di craned her neck to see. "Who signed it?"

"It isn't signed at all," Trixie answered, turning the paper over to see if anything had been written on the back. Nothing had.

"So now you know," Mart said, standing up suddenly. "I tried, and I failed to help. The whole Lonelyheart idea was dumb, and I shouldn't have started it in the first place."

Trixie looked up at him. "I still don't understand, Mart, why Sergeant Molinson should suspect you of anything."

Mart looked down at his feet. "I've had to do really sneaky things, Trix, so that no one would find out that it was only me who was Miss Lonelyheart. Yesterday there were so many people around the journalism department, all looking to see who was going to pick up Miss Lonelyheart's mail, that I had to leave it there. I sneaked back last night on my bike to get it. One of the kids must've seen me there and told the police this morning. That's the way it happened."

Trixie gasped. "So that's where you were!"

Mart nodded. "And when Sergeant Molinson asked me about it—"

Brian looked at him with sudden understanding. "You lied about it."

Mart's face flushed. "Yeah, I did. Real dumb, huh? But if I'd admitted being on the school grounds, I'd have had to say what I was doing there. And not only that, I'd have had to tell the police what I suspected."

Dan stared at him. "Then why didn't you?"

Mart held out his hand, then let it drop to his side helplessly. "Because I've got no proof," he said. "No proof at all. *I* think the person who's been writing to me is the same one who vandalized the school—"

"—and Wimpy's, too," Trixie added.

"And it could be any one of half a dozen people," Mart said, nodding. "I've been watching so many kids these days that I can't see straight anymore. You know the people I think it *could* be, but I can't watch them all now."

"So you want the Bob-Whites to help?" Brian asked.

"Of course he does," Trixie answered for Mart. "And I'm going to do all *I* can."

"Me, too," Honey added quickly.

Jim looked at the circle of solemn faces. "I guess that goes for all of us. When one Bob-White's in trouble—"

"It's up to the rest of us to help," Di said, nodding her head.

"Then the only thing now," Trixie put in, "is to decide exactly what we're going to do."

Dan frowned. "I still think Mart should tell Sergeant Molinson everything he knows about this."

"Aw, let's try it this way first," Mart said, almost pleading. "Then if it doesn't work—well— I'll be the first to admit it and go tell the police what I know. Okay?"

In the end, they took a vote on it. The final result was six to one in favor of the Bob-Whites trying to find out the identity of the Midnight Marauder themselves.

Dan gave in with good grace. "Okay," he said, "I guess I'll have to go along with what you've decided. But I still think you're wrong, you know."

"Jeepers!" Trixie said to Honey, as they made their way to the family room, "I'm sure glad we've got that settled. Wow! What a day! First I thought Reddy was missing—" She broke off and looked around at Di. "Speaking of Reddy, where is he? I expected him to come barking and running to meet us when we arrived."

Di pushed back her long hair. "Oh," she said vaguely, "I'm sure he's around here somewhere. Wait a sec, I'll find Harrison and ask him. He was the one who saw the two dogs earlier, anyway."

In another few moments, Di was back, and Trixie stiffened with alarm when she saw the expression on her friend's face.

"Oh, Trixie," Di wailed, "I don't know how you're ever going to forgive me. Reddy and Patch aren't here, after all! Harrison saw them first thing this morning—at least, he saw Reddy, and he assumed Patch was with him."

"But where did Harrison see Reddy?" Trixie asked in a tight voice, though she sensed Di's answer even before she heard it.

"He saw Reddy in the woods," Di said slowly. "It was about a mile from Mr. Lytell's store, and just off Glen Road."

Brian stared. "But we've already looked for Reddy there," he said, "and what everyone's been seeing is just an old scrap of someone's torn shirt."

"So I was right all along," Trixie said, her lips quivering, "and Reddy's *still* missing—and he's been missing all night."

Honey moved at once to her friend's side. "Don't worry, Trix," she said quickly. "We'll find him—you'll see."

"We'll get the horses now," Brian said, "and we won't stop searching till we discover what's going on."

"Is that okay with you, Trix?" Mart asked.

But Trixie was no longer there. She was already out of the house and running down the hill and across the wet grass to the Wheelers' stable.

Dreadful News • 8

WHILE DI RACED for the paddock to saddle up her own palomino, Sunny, the other Bob-Whites hurried to catch up with Trixie. Then together they entered the stable's dim and cool interior.

At once, they smelled the familiar fragrances of saddle soap and sweet hay and heard the eager movements of the horses, who seemed to sense they were about to be allowed to stretch their legs.

Regan, who had been talking to Miss Trask at the stable's far end, hurried forward to meet the Bob-Whites. "I don't believe it!" he exclaimed. "You've actually remembered that horses need to be exercised."

But Trixie wasn't even listening. "Oh, Regan," she burst out, "you'll never guess what's happened. We thought Reddy was found, but he isn't. I know I asked you before, but have you seen him? We thought maybe he'd been around—"

Her heart sank as Regan slowly shook his red head. "I haven't any idea where he could be, Trixie," he answered. "I already told you that first thing this morning. Then, when I didn't hear from you again, I thought you must've found him."

"Patch is missing, too," Honey put in. "I thought he was with Jim. Jim thought he was with you—"

"No," Regan said again, "I haven't seen Patch, either."

"What's this about Patch?" Miss Trask asked, joining them. Then she listened patiently while Trixie explained.

"I'm sorry, Trixie," Miss Trask said quietly, when she had heard the whole story of the dogs' disappearance. "When you asked me about Reddy earlier, I thought he was off chasing rabbits somewhere. I told you so, if you remember."

"That's what everybody told me," Trixie said.

"I thought so, too," Brian put in. "But now we're not so sure. Trixie thinks something may have happened to both Reddy *and* Patch. It seems funny that they're both gone."

Trixie was almost dancing with impatience. She wanted nothing more than to rush to Susie's stall, jump on her back, and dash away over the fields, yelling for Reddy at the top of her lungs.

She knew, however, that first they'd have to get Regan's permission to take the horses on their search.

Judging from the expression on his face, it looked as if he wasn't going to give it. He was frowning. "I thought you merely wanted to exercise the horses," he said, a frown crossing his pleasant face. "But, of course, you're planning a search party—and through the woods, too, I imagine."

"But we'll be careful, Regan," Honey replied quickly, knowing that he was always fearful for the safety of his beloved horses.

"And if we find any places that could be dangerous to them," Jim added, "we'll tie them up and go on foot."

Miss Trask, dressed as usual in her sensible tweed suit, ran a hand through her short, crisp, iron gray hair. "Yes, we know you will, Jim," she said. "But you see, Regan is worried because he and I won't be here when you come back."

"That's right," Regan said. "We were just about to come and find you, Jim. I've heard of a couple of super horses for sale over in White Plains. Miss Trask has a couple of errands to do there, so we thought we'd go together."

"But that's fine," Jim answered, looking from one to the other of them. "So what's the problem? Dad and Mom should be home from their business trip by the time we get back—"

Miss Trask was shaking her head. "No, Jim. That's something else I had to tell you. Your parents just phoned to say that they've got car problems. They're stuck somewhere in New England, and Tom's stuck there with them. They won't be home now until Monday—or maybe later than that."

Honey sighed, and Trixie knew she was wishing that her parents didn't have to be away from home so often.

She also knew that Tom Delanoy, the Wheelers' chauffeur, would be disappointed by the delay. He probably wanted to hurry home to his pretty wife, Celia, who was one of the Wheelers' maids.

I guess we all want something we haven't got, Trixie thought. *Honey would like her parents to be home more often. Tom wants to get home to Celia. And I want to find Reddy. Oh*, why *can't things work out right?*

Regan must have sensed her impatience, for all at once, he gave in, as the Bob-Whites thought he would. "Obviously, you have to find the dogs," he said in explanation, "and just as obviously, you'll have a much better chance on horseback. But be sure, Jim—"

Jim grinned. "I know. Brush the horses and make them comfortable as soon as we get back and before we do anything for ourselves."

"And see that the tack is hung the way it should be," Honey murmured.

"Stirrups on leathers," Brian said.

"Girth thrown over the saddle," Mart added, "and the bridle on the hook right under the saddle peg. See, Regan? We know. You can trust us."

Trixie looked at him sharply and thought she could detect the deep sense of relief that her almost-twin was feeling. Although his troubles weren't yet over, it was as if his mind was easier, now that he'd shared his problems with his friends.

And his friends *would* help, once they had solved this other problem. Trixie knew that, without any doubt whatsoever.

Even while the Bob-Whites were hurrying to saddle the horses, Trixie was wondering where on earth they should begin to look for the two dogs.

Dan, who had been working just as hard as the rest to help ready the animals, suddenly confessed ruefully that he couldn't join them in the search. He worked for Mr. Maypenny, the Wheelers' gamekeeper, who had already given Dan the whole morning off for personal business.

"But now I've got to get back," Dan said as he helped his friends mount their horses. "Let me know when you find the dogs, though."

"I'm glad you said *when* and not *if*," Trixie couldn't resist saying.

"Hey, listen, don't worry so, Trix," Dan answered, looking up at her as she sat astride Susie, the little black mare. "You'll find Reddy, and Patch will be with him, you'll see. As for that other matter"—he looked up at Mart who was seated, as usual, on his favorite mount, Strawberry—"you can count on me to do anything I can to help." With a wave of his hand, he was gone.

Regan watched them as far as the stable yard, where Di was already waiting for them.

"Now, have you mapped out where you're going to begin looking?" Regan asked, still worried. "Those woods around here are thick, as you know, and it's useless scattering off in all directions unless you know where you're going."

Trixie wasn't quite sure where they were going, either, but she wasn't about to tell Regan so. Nothing must hold them up any longer.

"I know where I looked this morning," she answered quickly, "so now we're going to search where I *didn't* look. Come on, everyone! Are we ready?"

With a clattering of hooves, they were soon out of the yard and, in another instant, were cantering easily across the wet meadow.

Jim, who was mounted on Jupiter, the big black gelding, led the way. Starlight, the chestnut gelding, with Brian on his back, trotted easily just behind. Mart on Strawberry, Di on Sunny, Trixie on Susie, and Honey, who today was riding Lady, brought up the rear.

Around them, the air smelled fresh and clean from the recent rainstorm, though Trixie didn't even notice. She was deep in thought.

"Remember that time when we went looking for Di's missing butler?" Trixie suddenly called to Jim as they neared Glen Road.

Jim reined in his horse. "You mean the time you found the headless horseman as well?" he asked, grinning.

Trixie frowned. "Why don't we start looking around that path we've named Harrison's Trail?" she suggested.

"Why?" Brian demanded.

Trixie shrugged helplessly. "It seems like as good a place as any to start. Besides, I've got a feeling—"

Brian groaned. "Not another feeling!"

Trixie nodded. "I keep on thinking about it, Brian," she said, "though I don't know why. We passed that trail this morning, when we were in your car, and I thought then—that is, I *think* I thought—that is—"

Jim held up his hand and grinned at her. "Okay," he said. "Say no more. If you *think* you thought, that's fine with me. We've already wasted enough time talking. Harrison's Trail it is." He glanced around at the others: "If Trixie's got a hunch about it, chances are she's right. I've learned never to ignore her hunches!"

As they moved off once more, Honey leaned across to her friend. "Have you really got a hunch about this, Trix? Did you think you saw something? If so, what was it?"

"I don't know, honest!" Trixie replied. "But we've got to start somewhere. And, oh, Honey! Just think! Suppose I'm right."

On the other hand, a little voice said from somewhere deep inside her, *you could just as easily be wrong.*

But Trixie tried not to listen to it.

Five minutes later, Trixie had dismounted and was bending over the lower branches of a thorn bush. It grew by the side of the road and marked the entrance to the path that, she knew, led eventually through the woods to Sleepyside Hollow. Today, however, she wasn't even thinking about the events that had happened there, when the Bob-Whites had been trying to solve one of their puzzling mysteries.

Now her whole attention was centered on the long, chestnut brown tufts of hair that were tangled in the thorns like alien blossoms.

Gently, she disengaged several bright strands. Then she looked up at her friends waiting silently on their horses. "The hair belongs to Reddy," she said at last. "I'm sure of it."

Mart let out his breath in one long sigh. "Jeepers!" he exclaimed. "But how on earth did you manage to spot it from a moving car?"

"I was just wondering the same thing," Brian said, staring at Trixie as if he'd never seen her before.

In spite of her worry, Trixie managed a weak grin. "I don't know how I saw it," she answered. "In fact, I didn't even realize I had."

"Maybe her cranium—or the brains inside it—aren't so pea-sized after all," Mart said, teasing.

"I still don't understand," Di said, frowning. "What have those hairs got to do with anything?"

"I think," Trixie answered, "that they have to mean that Reddy came this way last night."

"Or this morning," Brian put in. "Maybe he came by here today."

"Whenever he came," Trixie said, "somehow

he must've scraped himself against this bush." She stared off into the woods. "But then where did he go?"

Suddenly Jupiter moved restlessly, eager to be on the move again. Jim held him firmly. "I'd suggest," he said, "that we split up in pairs and comb the woods."

"Good idea," Brian agreed, "but let's not forget our promise to Regan to look out for the horses."

"Who goes where," Jim asked, "and how shall we keep in touch?"

It didn't take long to decide. Brian and Mart chose to search the area to the west. Jim and Di wanted to search the area to the north, which would eventually lead them to Sleepyside Hollow.

"And that leaves the east for us, Honey," Trixie said. "If anyone finds anything, we can give the Bob-White signal to summon the others." She pursed her mouth, and in another instant, she was sounding the Bob-Whites' secret signal. *Bob, bob-white. Bob, bob-white.*

Trixie's hopes were high as she and Honey turned their horses toward the area they were going to search, and for the next fifteen minutes, she and Honey were silent. Carefully, they watched the trail ahead of them, always mindful of the horses' safety. They also watched for any further signs of Reddy's progress. But if there had ever been any, the rain seemed to have erased them.

Soon they were in a part of the Wheelers' game preserve that Trixie had never seen before. Dark, damp trails crossed and recrossed each other. Many ended in a tangle of underbrush. Above their heads, tall trees stretched upward to gray clouds, which seemed to be gathering once more.

"I don't know how I could have been so wrong about the weather," Trixie muttered, leaning forward to pat Susie's neck. "I thought it was going to be a beautiful day. Now look at it! If it rains again, old girl, both you and I are going to get soaked."

Susie whinnied softly and nodded her head as if she understood every word.

Trixie glanced around to see if Honey was still following her and found that her friend had pulled Lady to a standstill. As Trixie watched, Honey raised herself in the saddle and stared at something to the right of the trail.

"Take a look at that, Trix!" she called, pointing. "It's funny, but I've never noticed it before."

For a moment, Trixie could see nothing but more tree trunks and bushes, and another dim trail that seemed to wind toward a small clearing.

"Did you find something—?" she began.

At that moment, she saw what had caught Honey's attention. A dilapidated old shack, its door standing half open, stood off to one side. It looked as if it had been abandoned long ago.

"I didn't know that was here, either," Trixie said at last. "I'm going to take a look. Are you coming?"

Without waiting for an answer, she slipped quickly from Susie's back and looped the little mare's reins over a low-hanging tree branch.

She heard Honey whisper urgently, "Wait for me, Trix. Someone might be in there. Oh, be careful!"

When Lady, too, was tethered, the girls crept closer and soon were standing beneath the old building's only window.

Trixie stood on tiptoe and tried to look through it. "It's too high," she whispered. "I can't reach, Honey. Give me a boost up."

As her friend obeyed, Trixie reached up and clung to the windowsill. She wiped the grimy pane with the heel of her hand.

Suddenly, her gaze sharpened as she stared down at the shack's dark interior.

Honey felt her give one startled jerk and heard her muffled scream.

"Let me down!" Trixie cried wildly. "Quick— let me down!"

Honey relaxed her grip and stared at her friend's white face. "What is it, Trixie?" she exclaimed. "What did you find?"

Trixie swallowed hard. "I—I found Reddy—and Patch, too," she answered, catching her breath in a sob. "They're both in there. They're on the floor. But, oh, Honey, I'm afraid we're too late!"

"Too late?" Honey echoed. "Trixie, what do you mean?"

"I mean," Trixie answered, the hot tears gathering behind her eyelids, "that I think both dogs are dead!"

The Letter · 9

DEAD?" HONEY GASPED, not believing her ears. "Oh, Trix, but they can't be. You must have made a mistake."

Trixie's teeth had begun to chatter. "There's no mistake," she answered. "Y-You g-go and l-look for yourself."

"Is there anyone else inside?" Honey asked, her voice low.

"I c-couldn't see anyone," Trixie said, her eyes filling with tears. "Oh, Honey, I don't believe it myself! What would Crabapple Farm be without Reddy? What'll I tell the boys? What will Dad and Moms say?"

"We're going to have to go in there," Honey said, nodding toward the shack's half-opened door. "We've got to find out how this terrible thing happened. We can figure out later what we're going to tell everyone."

Trixie struggled to stop herself from trembling. She knew that Honey felt just as sad as she did herself. She also knew that Honey could never enter that dismal shack alone. Trixie would have to go with her.

She took several deep breaths. "It's okay," she said at last. "I think I'm all right now." She bit her lip and clenched her fists as she took the first step forward. "Let's go."

Honey stayed close to her friend's side as Trixie reached out a still-shaking hand and pushed open the door. Two more steps, and both girls stood on hard-packed earth floor and stared down at the two bodies that lay there.

The two dogs lay on their sides facing each other. Patch, Jim's little black and white cocker spaniel, disciplined too late to be the hunting dog his master had wanted him to be, now lay with his tail stretched straight out behind him.

Reddy, his long, golden body looking like some bright banner, looked cold and stiff.

Trixie, the tears now streaming down her pale cheeks, dropped to her knees beside him.

"Oh, Reddy," she sobbed, bending low over his shining coat. "Why did this have to happen to you? How I wish I could bring you back! Reddy, can you hear me? Do you even care?"

And Reddy, as if in answer to her question, promptly opened his mouth—and hiccuped.

For a moment, Trixie thought her ears had deceived her. She stared at her dog's seemingly lifeless body. "Reddy?" she said, her voice quavering. "Did you say something?"

Reddy hiccuped again.

Honey gasped. "Why, Trixie, I heard that! Does it mean—can it mean—"

Trixie scrambled to her feet, hardly daring to hope that what she suspected was true. She stood over Reddy and gently nudged him with the toe of her shoe.

"Up, Reddy!" she ordered firmly. Then, remembering that he obeyed only reverse commands ever since Mart had undertaken to train him, she corrected herself. "Down, Reddy!" she said. "Down, boy!"

A quiver ran through the mischievous Irish setter's body. Then he opened one lazy brown eye and looked at the anxious faces bending over him.

In another second, his tail was thumping the floor with joy because two of his favorite people had come to see him, and soon he had scrambled to his feet and was trying to kiss both girls at once.

Patch, hearing the commotion, lifted his head and gazed with bleary eyes at the joyful reunion. Not to be outdone, he promptly joined in.

Honey and Trixie tried to hug both dogs at once. They laughed and cried and hugged the dogs again.

It was several minutes before Trixie remembered the rest of the Bob-Whites, who would, by now, be discouraged by their unsuccessful search.

"Will you call them, or shall I?" she asked, laughing as Reddy launched himself into her eager arms once more.

Honey's face was flushed with happiness. "I'll call them," she answered, and with Patch at her heels, she stood outside the shack and whistled to the wind: *Bob, bob-white. Bob, bob-white.*

At first, there was no answer. Then the wind seemed to send the message back: *Bob, bob-white. Bob, bob-white.*

After that, Trixie and Honey took turns sounding their secret signal to guide the others in the right direction through the woods.

As soon as they appeared, Trixie could tell from the expressions on their faces that they were fearful about what news they would find waiting for them.

Reddy and Patch, however, didn't keep them in

suspense. Recognizing the sound of the horses' thudding hooves, both dogs ran to meet their grinning owners.

"Hey, down, Reddy!" Mart yelled as his horse plunged under him. "I mean, up, Reddy! Up, boy!"

"For crying out loud!" Brian said, as Reddy turned his ecstatic attention toward him instead. "Why didn't you teach this dog to obey properly, Mart?"

But Trixie could see that her brothers were as relieved as she was herself that their dog had been found unharmed.

In all the excitement of the fond reunion, it was difficult for Trixie and Honey to tell their story. Finally, Brian asked, "But what were the dogs doing here in the first place? Did I hear you say, Trix, that you thought they were *dead?* What's going on, anyway?"

Trixie was silent for so long that the Bob-Whites wondered if she had even heard. Then she frowned and said, "I know what brought the dogs here. I'm fairly sure that they came last night. You'll never guess what I've just found inside that shack."

"I'll buy that," Mart replied. "What did you find?"

Trixie led her friends into the old building's dim

interior. "Look at this!" she said, pointing.

It took a moment for the Bob-Whites' eyes to become accustomed to the gloom. Then they saw what Trixie had discovered.

Against the far wall, a large cardboard carton had been tipped on its side. Around its edges were the marks of teeth—dogs' teeth. Inside the carton, a large, clear plastic bag had been eagerly ripped open, revealing several stacks of something round and red.

"Meat?" Jim said, puzzled. "Is it meat?"

"But not just any meat," Trixie answered. "They're hamburger patties, Jim." She picked one up in her hand and showed it to her friends. "There's enough meat here to feed lots of people— and a couple of dogs, too." She stared down at two unrepentant and tail-wagging culprits. "I'll bet this is what attracted their attention last night. They smelled it, you see. Then they got in here and stuffed themselves."

Di frowned. "But how did the meat get here?" she asked.

Trixie turned the carton around and pointed to the large letters printed on its side.

It read: WIMPY'S.

"I'll tell you how I think the meat got here," she said quietly. "I think it was dumped in this shack by the Midnight Marauder."

Five minutes later, the Bob-Whites were still discussing Trixie's puzzling find.

"I still don't understand," Di said, brushing back her long, silky hair. "What do you think the dogs were doing here? What were they doing on the floor like that?"

Jim chuckled and bent to fondle Patch's eager head. "These rascals," he said, "must have smelled the meat. Either that, or they saw the person with it and followed whoever it was. In any case, the dogs arrived here and promptly got to work on Wimpy's carton. Then, I would imagine, they had a feast."

"That's what I think, too," Trixie put in. "And I also think they ate so much they had to sleep it off."

"So that's what they were doing when we found them," Honey murmured.

Brian had thought of something else. "We'd better leave everything just the way we found it," he said. "The police will want to see this."

"Oh, Brian, do we have to tell them?" Trixie cried. "I thought we could do all the investigating ourselves."

Jim looked stern. "We can't do that, Trix. This is evidence."

"I don't care what it is," Trixie answered, her eyes flashing. "If we tell Sergeant Molinson about it, I know exactly what he's going to say. He'll think that Mart is the Midnight Marauder, that *he* stashed the hamburger here, and that we're trying to cover up for him."

"I think Trixie's right," Honey said in a low voice. "Couldn't we—?"

But Brian was shaking his head. "No," he said, sounding regretful, "I don't think we can."

"And besides," Mart said suddenly, as if he'd just made up his mind about something, "there's no way that Dad and Moms will let us keep quiet about it." He looked at his sister. "I'm going to tell them everything as soon as they get back."

"About Miss Lonelyheart, too?" Trixie asked, trying not to smile.

Mart sighed. "About Miss Lonelyheart, too," he answered, nodding his head, "though I'm not looking forward to that bit."

"Maybe I'm wrong," Di put in slowly, "but have you decided *exactly* what we're going to tell the police? I mean, we don't even know where we are. Trixie and Honey found this old shack by accident—"

"—and we merely followed their signals," Brian added, frowning. "How about it, Jim? You're the woodsman. What directions do we give the police, anyway?"

Trixie was hoping that Jim wouldn't know the

exact location of the old shack in the woods any more than she did.

But in the next moment, her heart sank as the Bob-Whites followed him outside while he explained. "If you follow that trail," he pointed to the back of the clearing, "it'll lead us to the Albany Post Road. Behind us is Sleepyside Hollow. And, of course, if we go back the way we came, we'll come to Harrison's Trail and eventually home."

"Speaking of home," Brian said, looking up at the black clouds gathering overhead, "I think we'd better get back fast. We can phone Sergeant Molinson as soon as we've seen to the horses, Don't you think so, Trix?"

But Trixie's gaze had followed Jim's pointing finger. "Are you sure we're close to the Albany Post Road, Jim?" she asked.

"I'm sure," Jim answered. "Why?"

"I keep on wondering," Trixie said, "why that hamburger meat was put in here in the first place. Why this shack? Why these woods? I wonder if the Midnight Marauder lives around here somewhere."

"Will you listen to her?" Brian said, grinning. "She's never satisfied. If we answer one question, she can think of ten more to take its place."

"At least we found the dogs," Di said, bending again to give Reddy a hug.

"Yes," Trixie said slowly, "we found the dogs. But I'd like to know if they found the meat by accident—or if they actually saw the person who hid it here." She stared at Reddy and wished he could talk.

But Reddy merely sat back on his haunches and looked smug.

It began to rain again just as the Bob-Whites were turning into the stable yard.

Di, who wanted to hurry home to care for her horse, waved a cheery hand at her friends and turned Sunny's head toward the paddock.

"You'd better hurry," she called over her shoulder. "Something tells me the weather's going to get much worse than this."

The words were no sooner out of her mouth than the stinging rain, accompanied by squalls of gusty wind, fell on humans and animals alike.

The Bob-Whites waited only long enough to see Di reach the top of the hill, and then they, too, hurried their horses into the safety of the warm and familiar stable.

For the next hour, Trixie was kept so busy that she had no time to think of the puzzling events that had taken place since she got out of bed that morning.

Jim, remembering his promise to Regan to look

after the horses, was taking his responsibilities seriously. He saw to it that each animal was dried, brushed, and fed, and he stood over each Bob-White until the shining tack was rehung on the stable wall, the way Regan liked it.

"Whew!" Honey gasped, her face red from exertion. "What a slave driver you turned out to be, Jim!"

Her brother grinned and ran his hand through his red hair. "I know," he answered, "but at least Regan can't say we didn't look after things while he was away."

A sound from the open doorway made him turn sharply, but it was only the wind, which seemed to have suddenly grown in intensity.

Brian moved to stare at the now-pelting rain. "Did anyone listen to the weather forecast today?" he asked, frowning. "Somehow I don't like the look of this."

"I sure didn't listen," Trixie called to him as she patted a contented Susie's soft nose. "I thought we were going to have terrific weather."

The boys weren't listening. Brian, Mart, and Jim were hurrying now to make sure that everything was secure.

Trixie heard Mart say, "Do you think we've got problems, Brian?"

"*We* haven't," she heard Brian answer. "But

I'm just wondering whether Dad and Moms are going to be able to make it home tonight, after all. If that road from Albany gets washed out again, they'll never get through. This rain doesn't show any sign of letting up. If you ask me, I think we're in for a real storm."

Trixie and Honey exchanged worried glances.

"Maybe," Honey said slowly, "Miss Trask and Regan will decide to stay over in White Plains, too, Trix. If they do—and if your parents can't get home, either—maybe you'd all like to come and spend the night at the Manor House."

But when she repeated her invitation to Brian, he shook his head regretfully. "We'd better not, Honey, thanks all the same. Trixie can stay if she likes. But Mart and I had better get back to keep an eye on things at home."

Mart nodded. "And don't forget, we've got to phone Sergeant Molinson, too—though I can't see him driving out to that shack in all this rain. And we promised to let Dan know when we found the dogs."

"I'd almost forgotten about Sergeant Molinson," said Trixie, who hadn't forgotten for even a moment.

She'd been hoping against hope that it was her brothers who'd forgotten their intention of calling the police.

"You don't have to be there, Trix," Mart said, his eyes watching her face. "In fact, it might be better if you weren't."

Brian chuckled. "It would be much better. I can see it all now. Trixie would be arguing so hard and insisting so hard on Mart's innocence that Sergeant Molinson would be convinced Mart was guilty."

Trixie hesitated. Maybe it would be better if she wasn't there. In that way, the sergeant couldn't forbid her to investigate on her own.

She looked down at Reddy, who lay comfortably at her feet, his chin on his paws, his eyes closed.

"Will you look after Reddy if I do stay over at Honey's house?" she asked.

Mart understood at once what she meant, and laughed. "Don't worry, Trix," he told her. "Our dog's not going roaming any more today. We'll keep our optic orbs focused firmly on the canine. You can count on it."

He bent down to Reddy, who opened one sleepy brown eye. "And no more hamburgers for you tonight, either," Mart said loudly. "You've had enough to feed a zoo! Understand, dog?"

Reddy yawned widely and closed his eye. He wanted nothing more than to take another long, satisfying nap.

At the storm's first brief lull, however, he was yanked unceremoniously to his feet, and a moment later, he was trotting sleepily after Trixie's brothers as they raced toward Crabapple Farm.

Jim took one last look around the stables, then hurried to close the big doors. "I'll come back later to check on the horses," he muttered. "Meantime, we'd better make a run for it ourselves. Are you ready? Ready, Patch, old boy? Quick, then! Let's go!"

With Patch racing at their heels, they hurried as fast as they could up the hill, while the wind tore at their clothing and the ice-cold rain stung their faces.

Once inside the warm haven of the Manor House, they saw Celia Delanoy, who seemed to have been waiting for them. "Oh, I'm so glad you're home," she exclaimed. "And you've found Patch! Miss Trask told me he was missing. Where was he?"

"It's a long story," Jim said, stripping off his wet jacket, "and we'll tell you about it later. Right now we'd better get on upstairs and climb into some dry clothes. Is there any word from Regan or Miss Trask?"

Celia shook her head. "No, they haven't called, so maybe they'll be home soon."

The three Bob-Whites were halfway up the

stairs when Celia seemed to remember something. "Oh, I almost forgot," she said, pulling a letter from her apron pocket and holding it up to Jim. "This arrived in the afternoon mail. I was going to give it to Miss Trask, but maybe you'd better open it, as long as she isn't here."

Jim frowned as he stared at the envelope. "That's funny," he said. "It's not addressed to anybody in particular. It says: Manor House, Glen Road, Sleepyside-on-the-Hudson. And it's written in block capital letters."

Trixie held her breath as Jim ripped open the envelope. She had a sudden suspicion concerning what he would find inside it.

Jim read the letter, then stared up at the two girls in consternation. "It says: 'Beware! Tonight I'm going to visit *you!*' And it's signed—"

"The Midnight Marauder," Trixie finished.

A Mysterious Figure · 10

HONEY'S EYES were wide with alarm. "The Midnight Marauder's coming here?"

Jim nodded slowly. "That's what the letter says. The next question is: What are we going to do now?"

Trixie leaned over the banister rail to see if Celia was still there. But the Wheelers' pretty maid had already hurried back to the kitchen and had no suspicion that anything was wrong.

Trixie was thinking fast as she hurried into Honey's bedroom and turned to face her friends, who had followed her.

"Listen," Trixie said excitedly, "I've got an

idea. Don't you see—this is our chance. It's what we've been waiting for. This time we know for sure where the Midnight Marauder's going to strike next. He's coming here. And when he does, we're going to catch him!"

Honey frowned. "I—I don't think I like it, Trix," she said uncertainly, and her hazel eyes were troubled as she gazed at her friend.

"I agree," Jim said quietly. "I don't think there's any argument this time. We're going to have to call in the police. We can't handle this ourselves."

"But we don't have to," Trixie exclaimed, brushing her wet curls away from her damp forehead with an impatient hand. "Don't you see? We'll call all the Bob-Whites together. Then all of us will stand on guard all night."

"The Midnight Marauder may not show up, anyway," Jim said suddenly. "Listen to that storm! I can't see anyone setting out in it. Anyway, what's the purpose in all of this?"

"I don't know," Trixie answered. "The more I think about it, the more it seems as if someone's angry—or upset—or—oh, who can tell? But this is our big chance to catch whoever it is. And it's our big chance to clear Mart's name."

Honey shook her head. "I'm sorry, Trix, I really am. I want to help Mart as much as anyone does."

"Well, then?" Trixie demanded.

"Oh, Trixie," Honey wailed, "you know that Miss Trask would never let us try to act on our own."

"But Miss Trask isn't here," Trixie pointed out, "and if this storm keeps up, I don't think she will be."

There was silence as the three gazed at each other.

"I'll tell you what, Trix," Jim said at last. "Let me call the police and see what they have to say. Maybe you're right. Maybe the storm's so bad that no one can get through. If that's the case, then we'll stand guard here ourselves. Okay?"

Trixie couldn't pretend that she wasn't disappointed. With Sergeant Molinson at the Manor House, there was no knowing what would happen. And suppose he stationed his police officers all around the grounds. In that way, he might catch the Midnight Marauder. On the other hand, Trixie had an idea that the mysterious intruder might be frightened away.

She sighed. "Okay, Jim," she said finally. "If that's what you and Honey want to do, I guess I can't stop you."

After he had gone, Honey squeezed her friend's arm. "Come on, Trix," she said. "Don't be angry with us. Everything'll turn out all right, you'll see. The storm is making you upset."

"I'm not angry," Trixie answered, trying to smile. "I understand how you and Jim feel." She sighed. "I guess if I'd been the one to receive the letter, I'd feel the same way. You're right, Honey. The storm is making me feel uncomfortable."

Honey looked relieved. "In that case, why don't you get out of those wet things?" she suggested. "You left a pair of your jeans here last time you spent the night. And you can borrow one of my blouses. How's that?"

Both Trixie and Honey had showered and changed by the time Jim returned. He knocked on the door and stuck his red head into the room. "You can relax, Trix," he said slowly. "It looks as if you're getting your own way, after all."

Trixie had been busy toweling her hair dry. Now she looked up, puzzled. "What do you mean?"

"I mean," Jim replied, "that the telephone lines have been knocked out by the storm. I can't get through to the police."

Honey paused with her hair brush in her hand. "But that means—"

Jim nodded. "It means that we're cut off from everyone, Honey. The storm outside is even worse than it was before. We're going to have to deal with the Midnight Marauder alone!"

Several times during the course of that evening, Trixie realized that things weren't turning out exactly the way she had imagined they would. She had hoped that the other Bob-Whites would be there to help them, and she and Jim had made several attempts to phone them. But it was no use.

Outside, the wind and the rain combined to thwart any ideas they might have had of running to anyone for help.

Several times, Trixie had run to the front door and opened it just a little way. She had gazed across the verandah of the big house and tried to peer through the driving rain. She wanted to see if, by some miracle, her brothers had sensed that they were needed up there on the hill. But they hadn't.

Neither had Di nor Dan.

Each time, Trixie had returned to the large living room, where Honey and Jim had gazed at her questioningly. And each time, Trixie shook her head.

Jim had made one more unsuccessful trip to the dead telephone, when Trixie burst out, "Oh, let's face it! No one's going to come and help us. We're just going to have to watch out for the Midnight Marauder by ourselves."

"But there're only three of us!" Honey wailed.

"There're four—if we also tell Celia," Jim said,

nodding in the general direction of the kitchen, "or more than that, if we tell the other servants."

Thus far, the three friends had instinctively kept their worries to themselves for fear of frightening the staff. Now, however, they discussed the problem, wondering what was best to do. Finally, they decided to keep the news to themselves.

"There's no way Celia can leave the Manor House tonight," Jim pointed out. "It might be different if she were sleeping alone in the trailer. But with Tom still away with Mom and Dad, she was planning on sleeping here tonight, anyway—"

Honey nodded. "You're right, Jim. Let's not tell anyone."

Trixie sighed and thought of the neat red trailer, the *Robin*, which Mr. Lynch had once given to Trixie and Mart but which now belonged to Celia and Tom.

The *Robin*, which had once been the scene of yet another of Trixie's mysteries, was now parked in a clearing in the woods behind the Wheeler stables.

Honey must have been thinking of the *Robin*, too. She smiled at Trixie and said, "I think Celia's lucky to have such a nice place to live, though that trailer could be parked a million miles away from here, for all the good it'd do Celia tonight. She'd never reach it in this storm."

"And I'll never reach the horses, either," Jim said, frowning. "I hope they're okay."

Trixie listened to the rain as it beat against the windows. "I'm sure the horses are fine, Jim," she said, with more conviction than she felt.

"In any case," Honey put in, "there's not much we can do about it, anyway." She sighed. "Could someone decide how we're going to catch the Midnight Marauder if he comes?"

The three put their heads together and made plans. For the sake of the servants, Jim suggested that they should pretend to go to bed. They would stay in their rooms until the house was quiet and then creep downstairs again and meet in the cozy, book-lined library. From there, all three Bob-Whites would keep watch on the house and plan to jump on any intruder if he appeared.

Honey was not at all sure about the jumping part, and she said so as she watched her brother check all the doors and windows in the house before following the girls upstairs.

He paused outside Honey's room. "Don't worry about it," he told his sister. "I'll do the jumping, and you can do the yelling. We'll make such a noise that we may scare him away, or else we'll get the servants to help us tie him up. Just don't forget and fall asleep. Remember, it's eleven o'clock now. We'll meet downstairs in about an hour and then take our places."

"I won't fall asleep," Trixie whispered back indignantly. "This is the chance I've been waiting for. I just hope the Midnight Marauder's going to make it tonight, that's all."

The two girls watched as Jim quietly closed his bedroom door behind him.

"You know, Trix," Honey said, her voice low, "there's something about all this that really puzzles me."

"Only one thing?" Trixie asked, leading the way into her friend's neat room.

Honey sat on the edge of her bed and took off her shoes. "Why would anyone send a warning letter before committing a crime?"

Trixie frowned. "You know," she replied slowly, "I've been wondering the same thing myself."

Afterward, Trixie was never quite certain exactly what had happened next.

She knew that one minute she, too, had removed her shoes and was stretched out beside Honey. She even remembered staring up at the ceiling and wondering if Miss Trask and Regan were even now on their way home. But she remembered nothing more until she felt someone shaking her shoulder.

"Trixie!" Honey was whispering urgently. "Oh, Trix, please wake up and listen."

"Huh? Wh-What?" Trixie sat bolt upright and stared into her friend's worried face.

"You were asleep, Trix," Honey said, glancing over her shoulder at the windows behind her.

Trixie gasped when she looked at the clock on the bedside table. Its hands pointed to two o'clock!

"Gleeps!" she exclaimed. "I must have dozed off! How could it have happened? And where's Jim?"

"I think Jim's fallen asleep, too," Honey said quietly. "I'm afraid we all did."

Quickly, Trixie swung her bare feet to the floor and stood up. "I don't understand how we could have been so dumb!" she said. "And what is it I'm supposed to listen to? I don't hear anything."

"But that's just the point." Honey gripped her friend's arm. "I don't hear anything, either! There's no wind. There's no rain. The storm is over, Trix. And if the Midnight Marauder is going to visit this house, now would be the best time to do it!"

Trixie gasped. "You're right! And I've just thought of something else. Suppose he's already been here!"

She hurried to the window and pulled aside the crisp, white, ruffled organdy curtains and gazed out at the soaked landscape.

As she did so, the moon suddenly sailed out

from behind a dark cloud bank. It turned the dripping trees and wet grass to silver. It shone on Glen Road, which wound like a wet ribbon across the land.

It shone on a dark figure at the bottom of the hill. Whoever it was was moving noiselessly toward the stable and the helpless horses inside it.

At the figure's heels, there frisked a golden Irish setter whose long plumed tail streamed like a banner behind him.

Reddy!

The Marauder Strikes Again • 11

IN ANOTHER INSTANT, Trixie had grabbed her jacket and thrust her feet into her shoes and was running across the room. As she wrenched open the door, she almost ran headlong into Jim, who, still fully dressed, had been about to knock.

"A fine watchdog I turned out to be!" he exclaimed bitterly, trying to rub the sleep from his eyes. "I only meant to rest on my bed for a second—"

"But we're not too late yet, Jim," Trixie whispered urgently. "The Midnight Marauder's at the stable right now!" She clutched his arm. "I don't know how it happened, but he's got Reddy with him! Who knows what he'll do!"

"*What?*" Jim shot her one startled look and bolted for the head of the stairs.

A second later, Trixie and Honey were right at his heels.

Soon they were racing across the verandah and down the hill. They were still some distance away when they saw the dark figure wrestle open the stable doors. As they watched, he slipped inside. And Reddy, his tail wagging jubilantly, padded after him.

"Ooh, that dog!" Trixie gasped breathlessly. "Doesn't he know he's supposed to keep intruders out? Wait till I get my hands on him!"

Jim stopped their headlong rush by holding up his hand. "Listen," he whispered, "we know now that we've got the Midnight Marauder trapped. He's inside, and there's no way he can escape. If we're careful, we can surprise him easily."

"How?" Trixie asked.

"There's a coil of rope hanging just inside the door," Jim said. "As soon as we get inside, Trix, you hit the light switch. I'll grab the rope and jump on the Marauder and tie him up."

"I was hoping," Honey remarked, sounding scared, "that you'd forgotten that bit."

"It just might work," Trixie said, frowning.

"And me?" Honey asked in a small voice.

"What do you want me to do?"

"You can yell your head off if you like," Trixie answered, only half joking. "It might startle the Midnight Marauder so much that he'll give up without a fight."

"On the other hand," Jim said, "maybe the noise will arouse someone—perhaps even Brian and Mart. It seems to me we'll need all the help we can get."

"For now, though," Trixie whispered, "let's be quiet."

She could feel her heart pounding with excitement as they crept silently closer and closer to the half-opened door.

Inside, she could hear the horses moving restlessly in their stalls. She could also hear the soft, stealthy sounds of the intruder as he moved toward them.

"Are you ready?" Jim whispered, getting ready to spring forward.

"Ready!" Trixie answered.

It was the wrong thing to say.

The word was no sooner out of her mouth when something launched itself through the open doorway and hurled itself against her.

It was Reddy, who thought she had called him!

Uttering loud yelps of welcome, he tried to fling himself into Trixie's astonished arms.

Trixie, caught off balance, tried desperately to save herself from falling. She grabbed wildly for the front of Jim's jacket.

Jim, feeling his legs shoot out from under him, reached for Honey.

Honey, with no one to reach for, had no choice in the matter. She fell, and her friends fell with her, while Reddy, ignoring the sea of mud and thrashing legs, bent his head and bestowed wet, slobbery kisses on three outraged faces.

Suddenly, from inside the stable, someone pressed a switch. A golden path of light streamed across the yard. A second later, a dark figure stood in the doorway. His long shadow was motionless as he stared down at the three struggling Bob-Whites on the ground.

Reddy, satisfied at last with a job well done, promptly sat back on his haunches and nonchalantly scratched his ear with his hind foot.

"For pete's sake," a familiar voice said, "what's going on? I know that some people say mud is good for the complexion, but this is ridiculous!"

Trixie looked up at the dark figure, which had moved now to grin down at her.

"M-Mart?" she gasped. "Is that you? What are you doing here? And where's the Midnight Marauder? Did you catch him? Is he tied up?"

Mart reached out a hand and helped his friends

to their feet. "I don't even know what you're talking about, Trix," he said, leading the way back inside. "When the storm stopped, Brian and I were concerned for the horses. We came to check on them, that's all. Brian's gone around back to see that everything's okay there. What's all this about the Midnight Marauder?"

He listened while his sister explained all that had happened, while Jim ran for rags to help clean off the worst of the mud from the three of them.

When Trixie had finished her story, Mart shook his head. "The Marauder hasn't been here," he said. "Take my word for it. And the horses are fine, Jim."

"Did Dad and Moms make it home, after all?" Trixie asked.

Mart shook his head again. "I don't think anyone could've got through tonight, Trix. We couldn't phone Sergeant Molinson, either. The phones are out."

Honey sighed with relief. "Then we were worrying for nothing. I'd suggest our best plan is to turn in, and right now. I'm tired."

"I'm sorry, Honey," Brian's voice said suddenly from the doorway, "but there's something you've got to come and see first."

Trixie turned sharply and she caught sight of the

expression on his pale face. "What is it, Brian?" she cried. "What's happened now?"

"The Midnight Marauder has struck again," he said, gazing with wide eyes at his friends. "He's broken into the Delanoys' trailer!"

Five minutes later, the five Bob-Whites stood in the clearing and stared in horror at the *Robin*.

The intruder had wasted no time in trying to open the red trailer's little front door. He had merely taken a rock and smashed a window.

Large jagged pieces of glass lay on the wet ground. Along the *Robin's* once-neat side, black capital letters spelled out the words:

THE MIDNIGHT MARAUDER WAS HERE!

Even as Trixie watched, the letters were blurring and running into each other.

"It looks as though this message was painted only a short time ago," she exclaimed. "Look!" She reached out a hand and explored the paint with one finger. It was still wet!

Reddy, who had followed them, was exploring on his own. Trixie saw him suddenly stiffen. Then he growled deep in his throat and stared across the clearing at a distant stand of trees.

Trixie clutched at Mart's arm. "Listen!" she whispered urgently. "I think someone's there!"

"Who—" Honey began, but a warning pressure from her brother's fingers on her arm silenced her.

The Bob-Whites stood as if frozen, listening, and kept their eyes on Reddy, whose hair around his neck was bristling.

Reddy growled again. His gaze fixed on that same distant spot, he began to move softly, slowly, toward it.

There was a moment's silence. Then someone burst out of hiding and began running desperately through the trees and past the stable.

"Quick!" Trixie shouted. "After him, everyone! Reddy! Fetch!"

Surprisingly, Reddy seemed to understand exactly what was expected of him this time. In another minute, he, too, was racing across the clearing with the Bob-Whites close behind him.

Trixie had never seen anyone run so fast as the slim figure that seemed to remain so infuriatingly far ahead of them.

Trixie's legs were pumping at full speed, but still she could see that she wasn't going nearly fast enough to catch their mysterious visitor.

He had, in fact, almost reached Glen Road and the bicycle that was parked there, when Reddy, mindful of his duty at last, circled around in front of him and stood, legs spread, growling.

The running figure skidded to a halt and stared

in terror at the dog's bared teeth.

"Call him off!" he yelled to the Bob-Whites as they raced to capture their prisoner. "Don't let him bite me! I didn't do anything, honest!"

Trixie stared at the frightened figure who faced them. "I should have known," she said slowly. "So you were the Midnight Marauder all along. Look, everyone! It's Lester Mundy!"

Reddy's Prisoner · 12

LESTER DIDN'T TAKE his eyes off Reddy for a second. "I don't even know what you're talking about," he shouted, taking a step toward Trixie.

He stopped abruptly when Reddy barked in warning. Hastily, Lester stepped back to his original position and stood as if frozen to the spot.

"You'd better tell us everything," Mart snapped, thrusting his face close to that of their prisoner. "We know you're the Midnight Marauder. You were the one who vandalized the school—and Wimpy's—and the *Robin*."

"First, call off your dog," Lester said.

"Talk first," Brian replied sternly, "and then

we'll see if we *can* call him off."

Trixie hid a smile. Reddy looked as if he were about to tear Lester limb from limb.

The Bob-Whites knew well that the mischievous Irish setter wouldn't hurt anyone—but Lester didn't.

He seemed to be thinking hard. "It was like this," he began. "I happened to be riding my bike along Glen Road—"

"At this time of night—I mean, morning?" Mart asked, sounding incredulous.

"I couldn't sleep," Lester replied, not looking at anyone. "The storm was making too much noise. Then, when the rain stopped, I decided I needed some exercise."

"Go on," Mart snapped.

"I rode my bike this far," Lester continued hastily, "when I noticed someone hanging around the trailer. I left my bike here and went to investigate, but the Midnight Marauder was too fast for me. By the time I reached the clearing, he'd already gone. Then I heard you coming. I thought you might be part of the Marauder's gang, so I hid. You know the rest."

"I don't believe a word of it," Trixie said slowly. "For one thing, you couldn't have seen the trailer from Glen Road. Try again, Lester, and this time, tell the truth."

Lester sighed and shrugged his shoulders helplessly. "You're never going to believe me," he said at last. "I've known that all along."

"Try us," kindhearted Honey said gently.

"It really all began last night," Lester answered. "It was late. I was out jogging. Oh, I know what you're going to ask me next. What was I doing jogging at that hour, right?" He glanced quickly at Trixie, who nodded. "I—I guess you already know I'm not the most popular kid at school. Somehow I always seem to say the wrong thing at the wrong time."

Trixie remembered back to that morning when Lester had bluntly broken the news of Mart's trouble with the police. "You aren't always very tactful," she said.

Lester hung his head. "I know. But someone at school told me that in order to have a friend you have to *be* a friend."

Mart gasped. "You mean you *believed* that stuff?"

Lester stared. "What stuff?"

Mart recovered himself quickly. "Oh," he said airily, "I seem to remember reading something like that in that dumb Lonelyheart's column in the school paper."

"I didn't think it was so dumb," Lester answered slowly. "I thought it was good advice. But

I don't know how to be a friend, so yesterday—I mean, Friday—I joined the track team. Coach said I should get in shape, though, so—"

"So that's why you were jogging," Trixie finished.

Lester nodded. "I thought if I went out late at night, no one would see me and know what I was doing." As Trixie looked at him questioningly, he explained, "In case I'm no good, you know? I didn't want people laughing at me."

"That makes a change," Brian remarked. "In the past, you've been only too happy playing the part of the class clown."

"That's right," Jim added. "And what about that fool trick you played at Crimper's yesterday?"

Lester bit his lip. "It was my last one, honest! I couldn't resist it. I—I'd already told someone to be on the watch for something happening on Saturday—"

Mart moved suddenly. "Was that *you*?"

Lester frowned. "Was what me? What's going on?"

Trixie knew that Mart was thinking of the mysterious letter Miss Lonelyheart had received, which had worried him so much. Now, it seemed Mart's correspondent was none other than Lester Mundy!

"Go on with your story," she said quickly.

"What happened when you were out jogging?"

Lester began to tell them his story, and the Bob-Whites listened attentively.

Lester had been running along Glen Road, not far from the place where they stood at the moment. Suddenly he heard a small truck coming along behind him—fast.

"I guess the driver didn't see me until he was almost on top of me," Lester explained. "He swerved to avoid me, and as he did, something fell off the back of the truck."

"Did the driver stop?" Trixie asked.

Lester shook his head. "I yelled to him, but he kept on going. And you know what he dropped? It was a big cardboard carton. I opened it to see if I could get a clue to its owner. Inside, I found a big plastic bag. It was filled with—"

"Hamburger patties!" Trixie exclaimed, suddenly guessing the answer.

"You're right," Lester said slowly. "I didn't think it would hurt anyone if I took the meat home. After all, that driver didn't seem to want it. So I left the carton by the side of the road—"

"That must have been the one I found just before we started out for school yesterday!" Jim exclaimed.

"—and I carried that plastic bag over my shoulder all the way home," Lester finished. "I must've

141

looked like old Santa Claus. Then I put all those hamburger patties in our freezer."

Trixie stared at him thoughtfully. "What were you going to do with all that meat?"

Lester sighed. "I was going to have a party. You know, 'to have a friend, you have to *be* a friend.' I thought I'd invite some of the kids from school to come and share it with me next Friday. Afterward, I thought we'd all go on to the spring dance."

Trixie had already guessed the answer, but she asked another question anyway. "About that carton you found—did it have anything written on it?"

Lester nodded. "It said 'Wimpy's.' "

The Bob-Whites were silent, thinking about what Lester had told them.

"You'll have to give the meat back," Brian said at last, the stern note back in his voice.

Lester nodded and hung his head. "I know that now," he answered. "I guess I wasn't thinking straight last night. I didn't know that all that hamburger had been stolen in the first place. I thought it was someone from Wimpy's driving the truck that almost knocked me down, you see. I didn't find out till I got to school this morning—I mean, yesterday morning—that there was any such person as the Midnight Marauder."

"You still haven't explained what you were doing hanging around here tonight," Mart reminded him.

Lester explained. He said he'd returned to Glen Road on his bicycle, soon after the storm had ceased. He said he felt his legs needed the exercise. But Trixie had the sudden hunch that he had had something else in mind.

"Why, Lester," she said, staring at him, "I believe you came here to do some investigating of your own. Did you feel that Mart wasn't guilty of anything? Did you want to help him?"

Lester nodded, looking embarrassed.

"Well, I think that's nice!" Honey exclaimed.

Lester then told them that he saw a dark figure running down the Wheelers' driveway. The person, whoever it was, had stopped at the unexpected sight of Lester on his bicycle. Then, in the next instant, the mysterious figure had run into the woods on the other side of the road.

"If that's true," Trixie said, thinking hard, "then you must have got a good look at whoever it was."

Lester shrugged. "I did, but I still don't know who it was. The person was wearing jeans, a red flannel shirt, and a ski mask. After he'd gone, I got curious. I left my bike by the side of the road here, and I went to find out what he'd been up to." He

143

was quiet for a moment. "You know what I found. Then I heard you all coming, so I hid, in case you'd think I'd done that damage to the trailer. But I didn't! Now will you call off your dog?"

"But we don't have to," Honey told him gently. "Reddy got bored long ago. He's gone to sleep, see?" She pointed.

Reddy, who had collapsed on the wet ground, had returned to his favorite position. His chin was resting snugly on his forepaws, and he was snoring.

Lester's jaw dropped. "Then I could have run away from you, after all?"

Trixie nodded absently. She was busy thinking of something else. "Why were you buying black paint this morning?" she asked suddenly.

Lester looked embarrassed. "I thought I'd help out with some of the signs at school that need painting—the posters for the spring dance, I mean. I—I guess you could say I'm about to turn over a new leaf. No more jokes." He sounded almost shy about it. "I'm going to try to make more friends from now on. Ruthie Kettner is, too. She's going to help."

Honey gasped. "So that was why she was buying a paintbrush at Crimper's!"

Lester nodded. "We've got some of the other

kids to help, too. This afternoon we sort of formed a club. We're calling ourselves the Third Hand Gang. We thought if anyone was in need of an extra hand for anything, we'd provide it."

Trixie stared at Lester as he climbed onto his bike. She still had the feeling he wasn't telling everything he knew.

"Who else is in your club?" she asked slowly.

Lester grinned. "There's me, there's Ruthie, there's Marvin Easton and Shrimpy Davis—I suppose we could have called our club the Desperadoes. We've all been desperate, you see. No friends, no nothing!"

"But all that's changed now?" Honey asked.

"I hope so," Lester answered, and with a wave of his hand, he was gone.

"I don't believe it!" Mart said, staring after him. "He made it sound as if that Lonelyheart column really helped a lot of lonely people."

"Maybe it did," Brian replied. "Doesn't that make you feel better?"

"It might, if it weren't for one thing," Mart answered slowly.

"What's that?" Jim asked.

"I don't know if you realize it," Mart said, "but we seem to have lost all our suspects."

Trixie shivered as they walked back up the hill. The air was cold, and suddenly she felt very tired and sleepy. Worst of all, she realized that Mart was right. Where would they look now that they *had* lost all of their suspects?

So who was the Midnight Marauder?

A New Clue? · 13

By the time the long night was over, Trixie was so tired that she felt as if she were walking in her sleep. Afterward, she discovered that she couldn't remember much.

She did remember hurrying with the rest of the Bob-Whites to the Manor House to awaken Celia. She remembered Jim gently breaking the news about the trailer, and she remembered Celia's tears as she stood inside the *Robin* and saw the damage.

Chairs had been overturned. Two lamps had been deliberately smashed, and cupboard doors stood wide open. In the little bedroom, drawers had been ransacked and their contents dumped on the floor.

"It doesn't make sense," Trixie remembered Celia saying over and over again. "Why would anyone do such a thing?"

Eventually it was found that the only things missing were three pieces of inexpensive costume jewelry, and ten dollars in cash that the Delanoys kept in a cookie jar.

Trixie also remembered that Celia had insisted on wiping away the Midnight Marauder's impudent message painted on the *Robin's* side.

Both Brian and Jim told the Wheelers' maid that it was evidence. They said she shouldn't touch anything until the police arrived in the morning.

But Celia wouldn't listen. She didn't mind leaving the interior of the trailer for Sergeant Molinson to see, but the outside? Never!

"If I leave it," she said indignantly, "the black paint will dry, and then we'll never get it off!"

In the end, the Bob-Whites had run to fetch rags and turpentine. By the time they had finished, not a trace of black paint remained.

When Brian had covered the broken window with a stout piece of board, the *Robin's* exterior looked almost as good as new.

Later, Trixie had a vague memory of wishing her brothers good-night and plodding back across the wet grass to Manor House. She vaguely remembered undressing and falling into bed in Honey's room. She remembered nothing more for hours.

When next she opened her eyes, a thin stream of sunshine was shining through the ruffled organdy curtains and a bird was singing outside the window.

"My!" a brisk voice exclaimed. "So you're awake at last! We were beginning to think you were going to sleep the whole day away."

Trixie turned her head and saw Miss Trask smiling down at her.

Trixie sat bolt upright in bed. "Jeepers! Is it late? What time is it, anyway?" She turned her head and saw that the pillow beside her was empty. "Where's Honey?"

Miss Trask chuckled softly. "So many questions as soon as you've opened your eyes, Trixie? Yes, it's late. It's eleven o'clock. And Honey is downstairs waiting for you. Here." She held out a tall, frosty glass of orange juice. "We thought you might like something to wake up by."

While Trixie sipped, Miss Trask explained that she and Regan had arrived home two hours ago. "The work crews have managed to fix the telephones," she said, "and the roads leading into Sleepyside are now open." In answer to Trixie's questioning look, she added, "A couple of big

149

trees were toppled in last night's storm. They blocked the way, which is why Regan and I couldn't get home last night. And when we tried to call—''

Trixie nodded. "We guessed what had happened."

Miss Trask sighed. "We didn't buy the horses we went to look at, either. It was a wasted trip. And we would have been even more worried than we were if we'd known about the damage to the Delanoys' trailer. Honey and Jim have told us all about this dreadful person calling himself the Midnight Marauder.''

Trixie almost didn't want to ask the next question, but she had to know the answer. "Have you called the police?''

"Yes." Miss Trask moved briskly to the door, where she paused with her hand on the knob. "Sergeant Molinson has already been here. He asked us all quite a few questions.''

"And Mart?" Trixie asked. "Did he question Mart, too?''

Miss Trask nodded. "He questioned everyone, Trixie. I expect he'll want to see you later, too.''

"Has he gone?" Trixie asked.

"I believe so," Miss Trask answered. "I believe also that the boys have taken him to a certain shed in the woods." She frowned. "I'm not sure what they expect to find inside it.''

150

"Meat," Trixie said and explained about the hidden hamburger.

"I see," Miss Trask said thoughtfully.

. After she'd gone, Trixie sat thinking about all that had happened the previous day. So much of it simply didn't make sense. Who had vandalized the school and Wimpy's—and why? Who had stolen hamburger patties only to discard them in an old shack? Why did the Midnight Marauder warn everyone where he was about to strike next?

Trixie couldn't guess the answers to any of these questions, and she shook herself impatiently as she prepared to shower and dress.

Later, when she hurried downstairs, she found Honey in the mansion's library.

"Oh, Trix," Honey said, hurrying toward her friend, "I wasn't sure if we should wake you up or not—you were sleeping so soundly. But so much has happened."

Trixie nodded. "I know. Miss Trask was telling me. I did forget to ask, though, if my parents are home."

"No, but they've phoned," Honey said. "They'll be home later this morning. Brian and Mart decided it would be best not to tell them about all the things that have been going on while they've been away. They'll find out soon enough."

Something in Honey's voice made Trixie look at

her sharply. "Has something else happened?"

Honey had been holding something behind her back. Now she withdrew her hand, and Trixie could see she was holding the Sunday edition of the *Sleepyside Sun*.

"You'd better read what it says," Honey told her friend in a low voice. "Not that you can miss it. The article's on the front page."

Trixie took the newspaper from Honey's hand and flung herself into the depths of a soft and luxurious armchair. Honey stood behind her as she spread the paper on her knee.

Trixie drew her breath in sharply when she saw the banner headline, and her cheeks flamed with indignation as she read the words that followed it:

TEEN-AGE VANDAL SOUGHT BY POLICE

"What is wrong with today's teen-agers?"

This is the question that is being asked by all Sleepyside residents today.

A teen-ager, calling himself the Midnight Marauder, is terrorizing our town. Already he has senselessly vandalized our junior-senior high school and the popular hamburger place known to us all as "Wimpy's."

Windows have been shattered, certain items have been stolen, and black paint, announcing the culprit's identity, has been sprayed on both buildings.

Dr. Anton Sibolsky, noted child psychologist, stated, when telephoned this morning, "There is no question but that this is the work of a seriously disturbed teen-ager. He feels himself unloved by his parents. Therefore, he is attempting to take his revenge on society."

Later, a spokesman for the police, Sergeant Wendell Molinson, announced that several suspects are under investigation. He also said that he expected to make an arrest shortly.

The citizens of our town have a right to demand that action against these suspects be taken immediately.

What is wrong with today's teen-agers?

Many people believe that to spare the rod is to spoil the child. This reporter endorses these sentiments wholeheartedly.

Trixie gasped when she had finished the article. "Did you see who wrote this?" she asked.

Honey nodded. "It was that same reporter we saw in Crimper's yesterday—Vera Parker."

Trixie frowned, her blue eyes stormy with anger. "Did you read that bit about sparing the rod and spoiling the child?"

Honey nodded wordlessly.

"That didn't come from any expert," Trixie continued, "at least, not an expert on children. All Margo Birch knows about is antiques. It makes me so mad! And what does this mean?" She tapped a line of print with her forefinger: "Sergeant Molinson is 'expected to make an arrest shortly'?"

Honey walked across the room and gazed out the wide windows. "I'm afraid he made it pretty clear this morning, Trix," she answered in a low voice. "He still suspects Mart."

"But why?" Trixie asked, staring at Honey's back.

Honey turned slowly to face her friend. "Because Mart refuses to say what he was doing at school on Friday night. You know and I know that he went there to pick up Miss Lonelyheart's letters. But he doesn't want anyone but us to know that."

Trixie stared down at the newspaper on her lap. "Then it all comes back to what we said before, Honey. We're going to have to find the Midnight Marauder ourselves."

"But how?" Honey asked. "And where do we start?"

Trixie was silent for such a long time that it seemed as if she hadn't heard her friend at all.

Then suddenly, she jumped to her feet. "I've had a feeling all along that I'd forgotten something—something important. At last I've remembered what it is! Yesterday morning, when I was with Brian, we were looking for Reddy."

Honey frowned. "Yes, you told me."

"And I found a piece of material caught on a bush," Trixie continued excitedly.

"You told me that, too."

"But what I didn't tell you," Trixie said, "is that

154

it looked like, a piece of old shirt—a red shirt. Lester told us the Midnight Marauder was wearing a red shirt when he robbed the trailer."

Honey gasped. "Do you think the vandal tore his shirt when he was on his way to hide the meat he stole from Wimpy's?"

Trixie nodded. "I think we could go and take another look at it. I just left it where it was, you know. Maybe it'll give us a clue to the Marauder's identity—and maybe we'll find something else."

"Like footprints?" Honey said.

Trixie was already on her way to the door. "Like anything," she declared, "anything at all! After all, let's face it, Honey. This situation is getting desperate!"

A Fresh Suspect • 14

TRIXIE WAS SO EXCITED at the thought of finding a fresh clue that she didn't want to stop for anything, not even to eat a late breakfast.

"I'm just not hungry," she told Honey as they raced to pull on their Bob-White jackets.

Honey frowned. "I do think you should stop to eat something, Trix," she said.

"We haven't got time," Trixie announced over her shoulder, hurrying across the verandah and down the front steps. "Maybe the police have already found out what the Marauder was wearing on the night of the burglaries. Maybe they've even found that scrap of material. Oh, please hurry, Honey. We may be too late!"

"Are we going to take the horses again?" Honey asked, panting with the effort of keeping up with her friend.

Trixie stopped so suddenly that Honey almost bumped into her. "Gleeps!" Trixie said, running a thoughtful hand through her curls. "I hadn't thought how we were going to get there. If we take the horses, we'll have to listen to a lecture from Regan. He'll say the ground is muddy. The horses may slip and fall. We'll have to promise to clean *everything* when we get back—"

The same thought occurred to both girls at the same time. "Let's take our bikes," they said together and then laughed.

While Honey retraced her steps up the hill, Trixie rushed to drag her bicycle from the Beldens' garage.

One glance assured her that Crabapple Farm had suffered no damage from the night's storm. It also told her that her parents and youngest brother had still not returned, and neither had Brian and Mart. The old farmhouse had an empty, deserted look to it. It made Trixie long to dash inside, yelling at the top of her lungs, "Don't worry, house. We'll all be back soon."

But of course, she didn't. In the next moment, she had forgotten the impulse completely as she pedaled furiously along the Beldens' graveled driveway to meet Honey.

Soon the two girls were speeding along Glen Road, passing Mr. Lytell's store almost before they knew it. They caught a quick glimpse of the storekeeper standing in the doorway and waved to him briefly. But they didn't stop, though they could feel him staring after them as if wondering where they were going in such a hurry.

Trixie's eyes were fixed on the road ahead.

"Will you remember the exact place where you saw that piece of red shirt?" Honey asked, breathing hard.

"I'll never forget it," Trixie replied. "Everyone thought it was Reddy, you see. I wanted to believe he really might be somewhere close by. So Brian and I made a thorough search all around the area."

"Are we nearly there?" Honey asked.

Trixie nodded. "Yes, but I've just thought of something else." She frowned. "Suppose that piece of shirt isn't there anymore. Suppose it was blown away in the storm. It could even have got buried under leaves and dirt. I don't remember what I did with it. I could have simply dropped it on the ground— Oh, why didn't I put it in my pocket when I had the chance?"

"But you didn't know what was going to happen, Trixie," Honey declared loyally. "You didn't even realize yesterday morning that there was any such person as the Midnight Mar—" She stopped speaking abruptly.

When Trixie turned her head to find out why, she saw that Honey's eyes were staring straight ahead and had widened in horror. Trixie soon discovered the reason.

Without warning, another bicycle rider had shot out from a side trail immediately in front of them.

Even while Trixie backpedaled desperately in a futile attempt to stop, Honey was shouting, "Watch out! Oh, please, watch out!"

But it was too late!

Trixie had a brief glimpse of the other rider's startled face turned toward her. Wildly, she yanked at her handlebars and swerved toward the edge of the road.

Then she felt her back wheel skid uncontrollably on a patch of mud, while her front wheel slid obstinately toward the trunk of a thick spruce tree.

Seconds later, she felt herself falling, and the ground was coming up to meet her.

Trixie lay still, gasping for breath and trembling with shock. She was too frightened even to move. She had a horrid suspicion that if she did try to move, she'd find she had broken every bone in her body!

She felt someone bending over her and a voice, close to tears, repeating over and over, "Oh, Trixie, are you all right? Say something. Speak to me. Oh, Trixie, are you all right?"

Trixie groaned and moved first one leg and then the other. No pain. Nothing was broken. Gingerly, she sat up and stared down at her Bob-White jacket.

Someone last night, probably Celia, had sponged off the worst of the mud from the encounter outside the stable. Now it was worse than ever. Lumps of mud and bits of dead leaves and small twigs clung to the front of it.

"There, you see?" a man's voice said. "I told you she was all right. Nothing to make a fuss about at all!"

Trixie glanced up and saw Honey's worried face bent toward her. Behind her stood an elderly man, dressed, incredibly, in walking shorts and wearing a torn red flannel shirt. His thin white hair stood out from his head, and his bright blue eyes stared at her with almost clinical detachment.

"You were speeding, Trixie Belden!" he announced, gazing at her unsmilingly.

"At least I wasn't racing through the woods," Trixie retorted. "Are you all right, sir?"

"Of course I'm not all right," the old man snapped. "You scared the living daylights out of me, to say nothing of almost breaking your own fool neck. Now I suppose you're going to tell me you expect me to provide milk and cookies for the two of you."

Bewildered, Honey was looking from one to the other of them. "But we don't expect you to do anything of the kind," she protested, "do we, Trix?"

Trixie nodded her head slowly. "Oh, yes. I think milk and cookies would be the least we should have." She sighed and slowly got to her feet. She felt herself all over. "I'm okay, I guess." She stared sternly at the white-haired man. "But if I'd broken any bones, I'd have expected far more than cookies. I'd want chocolate cake, at least."

Surprisingly, the old man chuckled. "I might be able to find you a piece of chocolate cake, at that." He looked at Honey, his eyes twinkling. "You, too, girlie."

Trixie hid a smile at the expression on Honey's face. She guessed that her friend didn't like being called "girlie" any more than Trixie did. But Trixie knew that it was useless to argue about it. Trixie had tried many times before.

"Honey," Trixie said, "I'd like you to meet Grandpa Crimper. He used to own Crimper's

161

department store, you know.''

"Still do," Grandpa muttered, "except they won't let me run it anymore. They say I'm too old. Lot of nonsense! I'm as young as I ever was.''

"I'm pleased to meet you, Mr. Crimper," Honey said uncertainly. "I'm Honey Wheeler.''

"Call me Grandpa, girlie," the old man answered. "Your folks must be the ones who bought Manor House. Well, come on, come on! What are you doing hanging about? If you want chocolate cake, you're going to have to come with me to get it. I don't carry stuff like that around with me, you know. I don't know what's wrong with you young folks these days. Can't think for y'selves at all. Have to tell you everything." He glared at Trixie. "Are you coming or not?''

Trixie was limping slightly as she walked over to the tree to examine her bike. Its front wheel was hopelessly buckled, and its back one was even bent out of shape.

"Something tells me I'm going to have to walk," she said slowly.

"Do you good," was the old man's unsympathetic answer, "except you won't have to. I seem to remember I've got a truck parked around here somewhere, if only I can think where I left it.''

Trixie frowned. "I don't understand. What were you doing driving a truck if you were out riding

162

your bike at the same time?"

All at once, Grandpa Crimper grinned at her mischievously. "I fooled 'em back at the house," he replied. "When they weren't looking, I took the truck—and I threw Sonny's bike into the back of it, too."

Honey stared at him, fascinated. "Sonny?"

"That's young Mr. Crimper," Trixie whispered in her ear. "He's the one who's running the department store now. We saw him yesterday, remember?"

"Yes," Grandpa said, "Sonny didn't want me to ride his bike. He didn't want me to drive his truck, either. He says I'm not to be trusted with anything on wheels. Another lot of nonsense! I was driving before that boy was born! Well, come on! Let's not hang about all day!" He turned and began walking away.

"But I still don't understand," Trixie called after him. "Why were you riding the bike?"

"I wanted to see if I could still do it," Grandpa barked as he walked away. "And, of course, I could! Mind you, the stupid machine got damaged a little. . . ."

"Damaged a little" didn't even begin to describe the bicycle in question. When the two girls followed the old man across the road, they found the Crimper bike almost completely demolished.

It was a tangle of twisted metal.

"It hit a tree," the old man said in explanation, rubbing his long nose thoughtfully. "Good thing I wasn't on it, though. *I* had the good sense to jump off. Wait here, you two. I'll get the truck. Now, where did I park the dratted thing?"

Still muttering to himself, he hurried away and was soon lost to view around the bend in the road.

Honey frowned as she stared after him. "Are you sure you feel like going to his house, Trix? And are you really okay?"

Trixie rolled up one leg of her blue jeans. "I've got a couple of bruises," she confessed, "but other than that I'm fine." She stared ruefully at her bike, which was now propped drunkenly against a bush close to the scene of the accident. "I don't know what I'm going to do with those crooked wheels, though. I don't think they'll ever be the same. I wonder if they can be fixed."

"I expect Tom can do it, once he gets back tomorrow," Honey replied absently, still staring thoughtfully along the road. "You know, Trix, I've heard you talk about old Mr. Crimper before, but he isn't at all the way I'd pictured him."

Trixie chuckled. "Did you expect him to be an old-fashioned sort of person?"

Honey swung around to face her. "That's exactly it," she said. "I thought he'd look—Victorian,

I suppose—sort of like his department store. Very turn-of-the-century, if you know what I mean."

Trixie smiled. "I asked Dad about it once, because I remember thinking the same thing. Dad says that old Mr. Crimper is a very shrewd businessman—at least, he was. Many people in Sleepyside like doing business at Crimper's because it looks—"

"Respectable?" Honey said.

Trixie nodded. "And safe, and conservative, and unchanging. Even young Mr. Crimper sees the sense in that. He hasn't altered anything ever since he took over the running of the place. I wonder if he ever will."

From somewhere far down the road, they heard the sound of a truck's engine start up.

"Are you going to ask Mr. Crimper if we can stop and look for that scrap of material?" Honey asked.

"I don't have to look for it," Trixie answered. "I've already found it."

Honey's hazel eyes opened wide as she watched her friend reach into her Bob-White jacket. A second later, Trixie was opening her hand. Lying in the palm of it was a small square of red flannel.

Honey gasped. "It's the clue we were looking for. But where did you find it?"

"I was about to tell you that we'd reached the right place," Trixie said, "when Grandpa Crimper shot out in front of me. This clue was the easiest one we've ever found. I fell on it, Honey!"

Her friend was about to laugh, when she saw the expression on Trixie's face. "Is there something else that's worrying you?" she asked.

Trixie nodded. "Didn't you notice? Grandpa Crimper is wearing a torn red shirt. He's also driving a truck."

Honey caught her breath. "But you don't think—you couldn't think—"

"That he's the Midnight Marauder?" Trixie frowned. "I don't know. I can't be sure. Oh, I'm so confused. None of it makes any sense, anyway. Everything that's happened since yesterday morning seems crazy."

"Or the *work* of a crazy person," Honey told her. "Do—do you think Grandpa Crimper is crazy?" She spoke in a low voice, as if she were fearful the old man would overhear her.

Even Trixie looked around carefully before she shook her head. "I don't think so, but I can't be sure, Honey. My dad says he *has* got more eccentric as he's grown older, but—"

She broke off abruptly as the roar of an engine came closer.

Suddenly there was a shrill scream of skidding

tires, and a small truck hurtled around the corner. Trixie caught a brief glimpse of a figure at the wheel. He was wearing a red shirt, and he was grinning widely.

In the next instant, the truck was headed straight toward the place where she was standing.

The Next Victim · 15

HONEY SCREAMED and yanked at Trixie's arm.

At the last possible second, however, the driver swerved away from the road's edge and slammed on his brakes.

Trixie was still breathing hard when Grandpa Crimper clambered nimbly to the ground.

"See?" he said. "I haven't lost m'touch at all. I wish Sonny could have seen me. Can't drive? Lot of nonsense! Come on, you two. Get your bikes, and let's put 'em in the back."

Trixie was still breathing hard two minutes later as she scrambled into the front seat beside Honey.

"I thought you were going to run over me," she told the old man as he clambered back into the driver's seat.

"Then the more fool you, Trixie Belden," was all Grandpa answered, fumbling with the key in the ignition.

Suddenly, the engine roared to life. Gears grated. Tires squealed on the road's damp surface as Grandpa Crimper yanked hard on the steering wheel. The truck screeched into a wild, neck-jolting U-turn, and soon it was hurtling east along Glen Road.

It was the wildest ride Trixie and Honey had ever had. Honey hung on to the dashboard, and Trixie fumbled to cling to the door's armrest beside her.

They discovered very shortly that Mr. Crimper didn't bother to obey traffic signals. He made up his own. Twice he came to a stop sign, and twice he merely speeded up, stuck his head out of the window, and yelled, "Coming through!"

By the time he had turned into the Crimpers' driveway on Albany Post Road, Trixie and Honey couldn't believe they were still in one piece.

"I never thought we'd make it," Trixie told her friend in an undertone.

"I'm still not convinced we have," Honey answered in a whisper as she stared with wide eyes at the tall, three-storied house in front of her.

It looked like a Victorian mansion, quite unlike the neat frame houses that surrounded it. The Crimper house was built of yellow brick and trimmed with curlicue woodwork. Its wide front porch seemed to have been especially made for the two comfortable rocking chairs that stood there, and its lace-curtained windows appeared warmly inviting.

"Nice effect, eh?" Grandpa Crimper said, watching Honey's face. "Everyone expected me to have a house like this. So I built it myself."

Before Honey had a chance to answer, the front door swung open, and a gray-haired woman hurried toward them. She was followed by young Mr. Crimper, who began speaking as soon as he caught sight of his father.

"I knew it!" he cried. "I knew Dad had taken the truck! He sneaked it out of here as soon as my back was turned."

The gray-haired lady sighed. "Really, Earl," she said, looking at Grandpa, "why you do these things is beyond me. Didn't you know how worried we'd be? Where in the world have you been? We've been going out of our minds thinking of what could have happened—"

"Now, Mother," the old man interrupted, "I only went for a short spin, and see? I've brought you a couple of visitors. Trixie"—he glanced at her wickedly out of the corners of his eyes—"insisted on having a piece of your chocolate cake. And this other girlie is Honey Wheeler. Her folks bought Manor House. Remember that place, Mother?"

Trixie could tell that Grandpa Crimper had successfully diverted his wife's attention.

With cries of delight, she hurried to welcome them to her home. Soon she had shepherded the two girls inside and led them to the warm and fragrant kitchen.

It was soon obvious, however, that Grandpa had not managed to placate his son. Even though Trixie did her best not to listen, she could hear young Mr. Crimper's exasperated voice scolding his father. She guessed that the mangled bicycle had just been discovered.

Trixie and Honey glanced at each other.

"Is anything wrong?" Mrs. Crimper asked, glancing in the direction of the angry voices.

When Honey had finished explaining what had happened, Mrs. Crimper looked horrified.

"Oh, my dears!" she exclaimed. "Whatever must you think of that old rascal of mine? Lately, if it isn't one thing, it's another. And Sonny—I mean, Earl Junior—gets so worried about his father."

She had a worried frown on her face as she told the two girls that Grandpa had worked hard all his life. "But now that he's retired," she remarked, sighing, "it's almost as if he hasn't got enough to keep him busy. So he looks around for something to do—and usually finishes up getting into mischief. I often think he's gone back to being a small boy again."

Trixie couldn't help wondering if Grandpa's "mischief" could include vandalism. She had had no chance to compare the scrap of material in her pocket with the tear in the old man's shirt. Before she left this house, however, she was determined to do so.

Mrs. Crimper insisted on making sure that Trixie's injuries were nothing more than bruises. Then she sat both girls at the kitchen table and placed a huge slice of chocolate cake and a tall, frosty glass of milk in front of each of them.

Trixie felt guilty as she accepted Mrs. Crimper's hospitality. What would this nice grandmotherly woman say if she knew Trixie suspected her husband of being a thief?

Honey was apparently having problems with this same thought, because she seemed unable to finish her piece of cake.

"Aren't you hungry, girlie?" a voice roared at Honey from the doorway.

Grandpa strode into the room. A moment later, his son followed him. Judging from the expression on young Mr. Crimper's face, he was still angry.

"The girls are probably still in shock from the accident, Dad," he announced, the color still high in his cheeks. "Trixie, we'll see that your bicycle is fixed at once."

"Pah!" Grandpa said, seating himself at the kitchen table. He eyed the chocolate cake and then cut himself an enormous slice of it. "I don't see why you're making such a big fuss about nothing, Sonny," he remarked with his mouth full. "I already told you. Trixie Belden was speeding—and the other girlie, too. It was a good thing I came along when I did. If I hadn't, they both might've broken their fool necks."

As Honey opened her mouth to protest this outrageously unfair statement, Trixie threw her a warning glance.

"I'm sure you're right, Grandpa," she said meekly. "But for now, when you've finished eating, why don't you show Honey your jewelry boxes?" Then, as her friend looked puzzled, she explained, "Grandpa's been collecting them for years. Some of them are very old."

The jewelry boxes were also in a sad state of disrepair, as Honey discovered later, when she and Trixie followed the old man into the large

173

living room of the old house.

It was obvious that Grandpa Crimper didn't think so. As he opened the door of the glass-fronted cabinet, where each jewelry box was proudly displayed, he lovingly fingered each one before handing it on to one or the other of the girls.

"Some of these boxes," he said, "have quite a history." He reached out for a small black japanned box whose wooden lid was almost cracked in two. "This one, for instance, was once owned by a president's wife."

"Martha Washington?" Trixie asked, hazarding a guess. "Dolly Madison?"

"Nellie Murphy," Grandpa answered promptly. "Her husband was once the president of Sleepyside's Businessmen's Club."

Honey's face fell. She looked politely at the row of small boxes, some with peeling paint on their exteriors, some with tarnished silver lids. Only one caught her eye, as Trixie had known it would. "Oh," she said, reaching out to touch it with a gentle hand, "but this one is beautiful."

Made of delicate bone china, the small container was decorated with china rosebuds and tiny bunches of forget-me-nots. On its lid, a small ballerina wearing a white lace dress, with china arms uplifted, held a graceful pose.

When Grandpa lifted the beautiful box from the shelf, Trixie heard once more the tinkling tune she remembered from early childhood. Mart, who had once listened to it with her, had said it was called "Greensleeves."

"There's a tiny music box set inside the lid," she explained to Honey as they listened, enchanted.

Grandpa set the last box back in its place and closed the cabinet door. "I don't care what anyone thinks," he announced, "this collection is worth plenty."

Trixie frowned and thought that Grandpa was probably right. The collection *was* worth plenty—but only to Grandpa, not to anyone else. Or could there be another person. . . ?

"Did someone offer to buy it?" she asked.

"Pah!" Grandpa replied, sounding angry. "Sonny wanted me to get rid of the whole lot several weeks ago. He called in someone from New York —some antique dealer—a woman who didn't know what she was talking about."

Trixie thought of the dark-haired woman she had seen only the previous day in Crimper's Department Store. "Was it Margo Birch?" she asked.

Grandpa nodded his white head. "That's the fool woman. She told Sonny the collection was practically worthless. She offered me fifty dollars for the lot. When I found out about it, I told her I wouldn't sell any of it for even fifty thousand dollars. She came back twice to try and get me to change my mind."

"She must have wanted the collection badly," Honey remarked.

"She said she'd found a buyer who was willing to take it off my hands," Grandpa said briefly, leading the way back to the kitchen. "She made it sound as if she was doing me a favor. Fool woman!"

From the expression on Honey's face, Trixie could tell that she thought fifty dollars for Grandpa's sorry-looking collection was probably more than fair.

His son, who had heard the last part of his father's conversation, obviously thought so, too. "Now, Dad," he said sharply, "Margo Birch is a fine woman. She was trying to be neighborly, that's all." He glanced at Trixie. "She lives a few doors down from us, you see, and she thought Dad would be pleased—"

"Well, she was wrong," Grandpa broke in angrily.

Trixie was still thinking about old Mr. Crimper five minutes later, as she and Honey scrambled once more into the cab of the small truck.

This time it was young Mr. Crimper who had

insisted, to Trixie's relief, on driving them home. Honey's bike was safely stowed in the back. Trixie's bicycle had been left behind in the Crimper's garage. The bike, she had been assured once more, would be returned to her as soon as it had been repaired.

"Don't worry," young Mr. Crimper told Trixie, guessing her thoughts as he pulled carefully out of the driveway, "I'll see to it that Dad won't get his hands on it once it's been fixed." He smiled. "In spite of what you might think, I'm glad my father's enjoying himself. It's just that I don't want any harm to come to him."

Trixie nodded. "I guess I'd feel the same way if I were in your position."

Privately, she couldn't even imagine Peter Belden, her banker father, ever indulging in the kind of eccentric behavior that Grandpa Crimper did.

Gazing idly out of the truck window, she noticed how much damage the storm had done. Although the air smelled fresh and clean, the many fallen branches made the woods look ravaged. It was as if the branches had been torn off by some giant, ungentle hand.

Soon they were back on Glen Road. Then, as they drew level with the path that the Bob-Whites had named Harrison's Trail, Trixie's tongue felt dry and her heart skipped a beat.

Sergeant Molinson's police car was parked at its entrance. It probably had been there when they had passed the same spot before, although that time, Grandpa Crimper had been driving the truck so fast that Trixie hadn't noticed it.

Now she guessed that the sergeant and his men were still searching for clues around the old shed in the woods. She also guessed that Brian, Mart, and Jim were still with them.

At the sight of the police car, young Mr. Crimper slowed almost to a stop. Then he frowned and muttered, "No, I won't wait now. I'll talk to the sergeant later, on my way home."

Startled, Trixie glanced at him. "Has something happened, Mr. Crimper?"

Even as she asked the question, she had a sudden hunch what his answer was going to be.

He nodded his head slowly. "I wasn't going to tell anyone," he answered, "except the police, that is. And I certainly don't want my parents to hear about this. It would worry them both."

He removed one hand from the steering wheel and reached into the pocket of his jacket. "Take a look at this," he said. "It must have arrived in the store's mail yesterday. Somehow, though, it got buried under some papers on my desk. I didn't find it until I went there first thing this morning to finish off some bookkeeping. I didn't know what to do. I was about to call the police when you arrived at the house."

He handed her a letter.

Honey drew in her breath sharply as she recognized the hand-printed letters on the envelope.

"And you say this arrived at the store yesterday?" she asked.

Mr. Crimper nodded and looked worried.

The envelope was similar to the one delivered to Manor House the previous day. This time it said merely: Mr. Crimper, Crimper's Department Store, Sleepyside-on-the-Hudson, N.Y.

Even as Trixie unfolded the letter, she knew what she would find.

The message read:

BEWARE!
TOMORROW NIGHT I'M GOING TO
VISIT *YOU!*
     THE MIDNIGHT MARAUDER

"If this was delivered yesterday," Trixie said slowly, "then that means the Marauder is going to visit the store *tonight!*"

"I know," Mr. Crimper said briefly.

Trixie felt a surge of excitement. This was the big chance she'd been hoping for. The Midnight

Marauder wasn't going to be the only one to visit the old department store tonight.

Somehow, in some way, Trixie intended to be there, too.

Trixie Makes Plans • 16

TRIXIE WAS STILL THINKING about the letter when
Mr. Crimper stopped at the entrance to the Beldens' driveway.

"Will you two be all right if I drop you here?"
he asked. "I want to catch Sergeant Molinson before he goes back to town."

The two girls nodded and watched as Honey's
bike was carefully lifted to the ground. Then, with
a cheerful wave of the hand, Mr. Crimper was
gone.

He was no sooner out of sight than Honey turned
to her friend eagerly. "Well?" she demanded.
"Did it match?"

Trixie had been so busy making and discarding first one plan and then another that she didn't realize at first what Honey meant. She frowned. "Did what match? Oh, you mean this?"

She pulled the scrap of material from her pocket once more and stared at it absently.

"Of course I mean that," Honey exclaimed impatiently. "I knew you wanted me to look at old Mr. Crimper's jewelry boxes to give yourself a chance to compare the two pieces of cloth. I also saw you holding one against the other behind his back."

Trixie chuckled. "I didn't think you'd noticed."

"So did they match? Was Grandpa's torn shirt the one the Midnight Marauder was wearing on Friday night?"

Honey's face fell as Trixie shook her head. "No," Trixie said, "it didn't. It was the wrong shade of red. And from the way Mrs. Crimper was scolding just as we were leaving, I've got an idea that Grandpa's shirt wasn't torn when he left home this morning. Maybe it got ripped when we collided on our bikes."

Honey sighed. "I was hoping we'd found the villain."

"Perhaps we already have," Trixie said, still thinking hard. "Have you considered that it might be *young* Mr. Crimper who's the Midnight

Marauder? I have a hunch—"

Honey stared. "But why would you think so?"

"He does have a truck," Trixie pointed out, "and we know the vandal drove one on Friday night." She ran a hand through her curls. "I just can't think why he would want to vandalize his own store, though."

"Maybe to collect the insurance money?" Honey suggested.

"Then why did he also rob the school—and Wimpy's—and the *Robin?* It just doesn't make sense."

"None of it has made sense," Honey exclaimed suddenly, "ever since this business started. The villain, whoever he is, broke a window at school and stole only a small amount of cash. He stole hamburger meat from Wimpy's—and then he dropped it from his truck—"

"—and the rest he stored in an old shed in the woods," Trixie added.

"And then when he came to the *Robin,*" Honey said, "he stole three junk-jewelry necklaces and only ten dollars in cash."

The two girls stared at each other.

"It's almost as if he's just trying to be a pest," Trixie said at last.

"Or someone who likes practical jokes."

"Or someone else at school that we haven't

thought of," Trixie said slowly. "One of Mart's pen pals who've been writing to Miss Lonelyheart."

Honey was silent, and Trixie guessed she was trying to think which teen-ager it could be.

"The only one we know for sure *isn't* the Midnight Marauder," Trixie continued, frowning, "is Mart. And only we Bob-Whites are certain of that. This is why, Honey, we've got to be there tonight."

Honey looked startled. "Be where?"

"Crimper's," Trixie replied and then began walking along the driveway. "We've got to think of some way to get in there. It's Sunday, so the department store closes early tonight, at six."

Honey, wheeling her bike beside her friend, was already shaking her head. "I don't see how we're going to arrange that, Trix. Tomorrow's a school day, so we'll be expected to turn in early."

"I'll find a way," Trixie muttered. "I've just got to."

She frowned as she approached Crabapple Farm. Her father's car, which she had expected to see parked in the driveway, wasn't there. Neither was there any sign that her mother was home. The house was obviously still deserted—except for Reddy.

Suddenly he came bounding around the side of

the house toward the two girls. Then, when he saw them, he skidded to a halt and growled softly, deep in his throat.

Trixie looked at him in astonishment. "Reddy! What's the matter, boy?" She snapped her fingers. "Come! I mean—go!"

Reddy came at once, though slowly, as if he were reluctant to obey. Soon he was sitting at Trixie's feet and looking at her expectantly, as if he were demanding some sort of reward. When none was forthcoming, he merely appeared bored and soon strolled back toward the house.

Honey laughed. "I wonder what that was all about. It looked as if he was expecting someone else and was disappointed that it was only us."

In another moment, both girls had forgotten the incident as Trixie let them into the kitchen through the back door.

"I don't understand it, Honey," she exclaimed, looking around the familiar room. "Dad, Moms, and Bobby should have been home long ago. What could have happened to them?"

It wasn't long before her question was answered. The telephone rang just as Trixie was about to hurry upstairs to change out of her muddy clothes.

"Trixie?" her mother's voice said on the other end of the line. "Where have you been? Where are

Brian and Mart? I've been calling home every ten minutes for the last hour."

Quickly, Trixie explained that she had been at Manor House with Honey. "And the boys are around here somewhere," she added vaguely, not wanting to worry her mother with the details of where they really were—and what they were doing there.

Mrs. Belden hesitated and then said slowly, "The silliest thing has happened, Trixie. We were all ready to come home, when I slipped as I was getting into the car."

"Oh, Moms!" Trixie cried, her heart skipping a beat. "Are you all right? Did you hurt yourself?"

"I seem to have wrenched my back," her mother answered. "But it's all right. The doctor says it's not serious—except he says I should stay relaxed and quiet until tomorrow. Do you think you children can manage till then? Dad's here, and he wants to talk to you. Bobby, too."

Five minutes later, Trixie turned away from the telephone. Although she still felt concerned about her mother, Mr. Belden had assured her several times that the injury was not anything to be upset about.

"And we'll be home tomorrow, without fail," Peter Belden had said. "Tell Brian I'm relying on him to keep an eye on things for me. I've already called the bank and told them I won't be in until late tomorrow. As for Bobby, he'll have to miss a morning at school, that's all. It can't be helped. Now, are you sure you kids are going to be okay?"

Trixie had assured him that they would be. She had talked to Bobby, who sounded rather pleased at the thought of having a morning off from school.

"It's like a 'cation, Trix," his high voice piped into her ear. "Don't you wish you were having a 'cation, too?"

He'd sounded delighted when she assured him that she did wish she was having a vacation, though, as she told Honey as soon as the phone conversation was over, a vacation was the last thing on her mind right now.

"This is going to make a difference in our plans," Trixie said. "I wish Moms hadn't hurt her back, and I do wish they were home. But, Honey, don't you see?" Her eyes sparkled with excitement. "Now we'll be able to go to Crimper's tonight."

Honey frowned. "I don't like it, Trix," she answered. "It's sneaky. Anyway, Brian won't let you go."

Trixie stared at her friend thoughtfully. "He would—if I told him about it. But I don't think I'm going to say anything."

Honey looked at her friend with wide, troubled eyes. "That may be all right for you, Trixie, but what about me? Miss Trask won't let me go, either."

"I've thought of that," Trixie answered, moving once more toward the foot of the stairs. "You can tell Miss Trask you're spending the night with me. I'll tell Brian I'm spending the night with you, and then—"

"But that's sneaky!" Honey wailed, following her friend upstairs to her bedroom.

"I know," Trixie said quietly, turning to face her friend. "But think of it this way, Honey. Mart's in trouble—and with the police, too. He needs help. We've got to help him—at least, I have to."

Honey thought for a moment. "All right, I'll come. But I hope we won't be sorry."

"We won't be sorry," Trixie assured her.

All the same, she put her hands behind her back and crossed all her fingers, just to make sure.

Caught at Crimper's • 17

TRIXIE HAD NEVER KNOWN a day to last as long as that one did. She found herself watching the clock and wondering if it had stopped.

Honey had gone home to ask permission to stay with Trixie overnight, and Brian and Mart returned at last.

Trixie could tell from the expressions on their faces that there had been no new discoveries at the shed in the woods.

Mart told his sister briefly that he was still under suspicion. Then both boys listened quietly while Trixie explained what had happened to their mother.

Brian insisted on placing a call to Albany to hear for himself that Mrs. Belden really was all right.

Mart, too, talked to his parents. At one point, Trixie noticed, he hesitated before assuring his father that everything was fine at home.

Trixie could tell that he would have liked to tell his parents all his troubles, but he didn't.

"I didn't want to worry them," he said when he hung up at last.

"Quit worrying about it, Mart," Brian told his brother. "If you'd only tell the sergeant what you were doing at school Friday night. . . ."

But Mart flatly refused. Although he had felt better when, the previous day, he had told his secret to the other Bob-Whites, today he was blaming himself again for all that had happened.

"It's all my fault," he repeated several times. "I've obviously given someone rotten advice— and they've done what I told them to do."

"You don't know that for sure," Brian objected.

"Then, what other explanation is there for what's been going on?" Mart demanded.

"If it hadn't been for that dumb article in this morning's *Sun*—" Trixie began.

"It's more than that," Mart said, gazing at her miserably. "It isn't only the opinion of the reporter, Vera Parker, that counts. It isn't only Margo

190

Birch who thinks the Midnight Marauder's a disturbed teen-ager. It's the whole community. I was listening to the radio this morning. Since the damage to the *Robin*, everyone's angry and upset. They're afraid they might be the next ones on the list, you see."

Trixie opened her mouth to correct him but then hastily closed it again.

Brian hadn't noticed. "Everyone thinks the vandal is a student from Sleepyside's junior-senior high school, Trix," he explained.

Mart stared at Reddy who was sitting by the back door, waiting to be let out again, for the third time in as many minutes.

"Even Reddy doesn't want to be friends with me today," Mart remarked bitterly.

"He doesn't want to be friends with any of us today," Brian answered, watching Reddy race outside once the door was opened for him. "What's the matter with that dog?"

But Trixie had things other than Reddy's peculiar behavior to think about. Brian was taking his responsibilities seriously. As temporary head of the house, he insisted that all chores had to be done before their parents returned.

Soon Trixie was busy dusting, a job she disliked. She discovered that even this didn't make the time pass any more quickly.

Several times, during the course of that long afternoon, Trixie almost confided in her eldest brother. In the end, she didn't, because she felt sure Brian wouldn't approve of what she was about to do. If her parents had been home, it might have been different. With them away, Brian was being unusually bossy.

It was four o'clock when Trixie put away all the cleaning materials. Then she said casually, "By the way, Brian, I've been invited to sleep over at Honey's again tonight."

Brian was unsuspicious. "Don't be late for school in the morning, then" was all he answered.

Stopping only to snatch an old jacket from her room, Trixie raced out of the house. Minutes later, as arranged, she met Honey at the bus stop at the bottom of the Wheelers' driveway.

"Everything all set?" Trixie asked, making sure no one was watching them.

"I still feel guilty," Honey said, pulling her jacket closer around her. "I told Miss Trask I was sleeping over at your house. You've told Brian you're sleeping over at mine. I just hope no one finds out what fibs we've been telling."

She was still worrying about it when the bus arrived, and by the time they reached Sleepyside, Trixie was feeling just as guilty as her friend.

As she led the way across the town square, she

comforted herself with the thought that she and Honey had lied in order to help Mart.

"I still don't know what we're supposed to do now," Honey remarked as, once more, they stood outside Crimper's Department Store.

"But I do," Trixie replied. "I've got it all worked out. Don't forget, Honey, I've known Crimper's ever since I was little. I know of a place inside the store where we can hide. Then we're going to wait until the Midnight Marauder arrives."

"And what happens after that?" Honey asked.

"We'll figure that out later—I hope," Trixie replied.

Honey shivered and looked up and down the street. It was almost as if she expected the Midnight Marauder to appear right then. But all she saw was the usual number of Sunday shoppers.

Trixie glanced at young Mr. Crimper's glass-fronted office as they hurried into the store, but he wasn't there, nor did anyone show the slightest interest in their movements.

Soon Trixie had led the way to the creaking old elevator, and moments later, she and Honey were on their way to the second floor.

When they arrived, Trixie stepped out and looked carefully to her right. There, two saleswomen, deep in a conversation of their own, didn't even look around.

"Quick, Honey, this way!" Trixie muttered as she walked toward a stack of mattresses piled high along one wall.

Honey glanced at the array of bedroom furniture that now surrounded her. "What—" she began.

Trixie was tugging urgently at her arm. Wordlessly, she pointed.

Honey gasped as she saw, beside the mattresses, a small door. "What is it?" she asked.

"It's an unused cupboard," Trixie hissed in her ear. "It's not very deep, but it runs the length of the upper story. I found it once—oh, long ago when Moms was shopping and I got bored."

While she was talking, she had already grasped the handle and had pulled on it gently. It opened without a sound.

Honey glanced over her shoulder.

"It's all right," Trixie told her impatiently. "No one can see us. The mattresses are hiding us from everybody."

The space inside the cupboard was pitch black.

"Is—is this where we're going to hide?" Honey asked, knowing the answer.

Trixie nodded. "Come on," she whispered. "Follow me."

She had to bend almost double to get through the small door, but once she was inside, there was plenty of headroom.

She waited until Honey was standing beside her, and then she closed the door softly behind them.

When their eyes became accustomed to the darkness around them, Trixie could see old pipes and cables running along the outside wall. She guessed the space served as a storage area, too, though she could see little of the boxes around her. There was no light of any kind, and Trixie soon began wishing she had thought to bring one with her.

"What now?" Honey whispered through the darkness.

"Now we wait," Trixie whispered back. "We can sit on the floor and wait till everyone's gone."

"And then?"

Trixie sighed. "And then, if we're lucky, we'll be ready to catch the Midnight Marauder."

Even after the store was closed, Trixie insisted on staying hidden.

The hours passed slowly. Outside, there was no sound. The luminous hands on Honey's watch showed ten o'clock, eleven, eleven-thirty.

At last, Trixie eased herself quietly to her feet and took a cautious step forward.

"I think it's safe," she said at last. "We can wait out there by the mattresses." She opened the door cautiously and peered around.

Two small lights had been left on. They enabled

her to see that the coast was clear.

In another moment, Trixie had motioned for Honey to join her, and soon the two friends stood together in the big deserted store.

Trixie giggled. "We did it, Honey," she said. "No one even suspected we were there."

"I know," Honey replied softly, "but I've just thought of something else. How is the Midnight Marauder going to get in here? Surely he'll know the police are watching the outside and waiting for him."

Trixie caught her breath. The police! She'd forgotten all about them. Surely the Midnight Marauder must have forgotten about them, too. Why else would he have sent a warning letter to let everyone know where he was going to strike next?

She frowned. "You know, Honey," she said, "that's the most puzzling thing of all. The Marauder sent a letter to the school, *and* to Wimpy's, *and* to Manor House—"

"He wasn't taking much of a chance with the first two places he visited," Honey said, staring apprehensively at the dark shadows around them. "His letters weren't delivered until *after* he'd robbed both places. And he didn't really visit Manor House, either. He undoubtedly went to the trailer instead, and robbed and vandalized it."

Trixie stared at her. Honey was right! The Midnight Marauder hadn't taken any chances at all.

"But what's his purpose?" she asked. "What can he be after?"

Honey giggled nervously. "He's gone to so much trouble, he must be after a lot of money."

"But he hasn't stolen much money," Trixie said, thinking hard. "The most he got of *anything* was from Wimpy's."

Honey shrugged. "I don't know. Maybe he's just trying to throw everyone off the track."

Trixie stood as if frozen to the spot. "Oh, Honey," she breathed. "I think you're right again! Suppose you wanted to rob a particular place, but if you did, you'd be the number one suspect. So, to fool everyone, you commit *several* robberies to make it look like the work of someone else. And suppose it isn't the first three robberies that are important. It's the last one. *This one.*"

"You mean," Honey said, startled, "that he's been waiting to rob Crimper's all along?"

"Yes," Trixie said, nodding her head, "but not *this* Crimper's. Oh, Honey, don't you see? We're waiting in the *wrong place!* Quick! We've got to get out of here fast! It's our last chance to catch the Midnight Marauder in the act! If we fail now, Mart will be under suspicion for the rest of his life!"

Already she was hurrying toward the head of

the stairs. Then she stopped, her heart pounding. *Someone was moving about on the floor below!*

Trixie caught a glimpse of a figure sneaking along the center aisle. She saw a dark shadow at his heels.

Then, suddenly, everything seemed to happen at once. The store's wide front doors crashed open. Trixie could see the street outside alive with policemen. They carried guns.

"Hold it right there!" one of them yelled from the store's entrance. "We've got you covered!"

The figure stood stock still.

A burly man hurried toward him. "This time we've caught you, Mr. Midnight Marauder!" Sergeant Molinson sneered as he shone his flashlight into the intruder's white face.

And Trixie saw that it was Mart!

Marauder Is Revealed · 18

TRIXIE DIDN'T HESITATE for a second. She almost flew down the rest of the stairs.

"Trixie!" gasped Mart. "What are you doing here?"

"Wait! Oh, please, wait, Sergeant Molinson!" she cried wildly.

Astonishingly, the police sergeant *was* waiting, and in another second, Trixie saw why. The dark shadow she had seen at Mart's heels had now resolved itself into a long canine shape. It had bared teeth. It was growling menacingly.

It was Reddy!

Sergeant Molinson was motioning to his men to

stand back. Slowly, Trixie saw him lift his gun.

"No!" she screamed and flung herself forward.

She saw Sergeant Molinson's startled face turn toward her. Then he caught sight of Honey, who was hurrying toward them.

"Will you look at this?" he yelled. "Here's two more thieves we've caught, right in the act of robbing the place. I should have known all along that the Belden boy had accomplices."

Trixie didn't stop to answer. She lunged forward and took a firm grip on Reddy's collar.

"You've got to listen to me!" she cried desperately. "If you don't—" her mind searched wildly for an effective threat—"I'll turn my dog loose on all of you. And I've got to warn you, he's a killer!"

Immediately, Reddy stopped growling. His back legs collapsed under him, and he sat there, wagging his tail. He gazed warmly at Sergeant Molinson and looked the picture of innocence.

Mart didn't notice. "I didn't do anything, Trix," he said. "I heard young Mr. Crimper telling the police about the letter he'd received, that's all. I decided to try and catch the Midnight Marauder myself. I must have left home just before you did. I came here on my bike. Reddy followed me, but I didn't notice him till I was almost into town. We've been hiding in one of the storage cupboards back there."

Trixie didn't give Sergeant Molinson a chance to say anything. Hurriedly, with a worried look at the large clock on the wall, she told the sergeant her suspicions.

Even Mart was surprised when he realized that his sister had worked out the identity of the Midnight Marauder.

"So you see," Trixie finished at last, "we haven't got a moment to lose. We've got to get over there *at once*, before the next robbery takes place."

Sergeant Molinson's face turned redder than ever. "And you expect me to swallow that yarn?" he asked, grinning over his shoulder at his men. "Nothin' doin', kid. Come on, now, you're coming to the police station with me. And if that dog so much as moves—" He made a threatening gesture toward the gun still clenched in his beefy fist.

Reddy was oblivious to the danger. He sat, still thumping the floor with his tail, and gazed soulfully at all of them.

Afterward, Trixie wasn't sure what would have happened if there hadn't been a sudden disturbance at the entrance.

In the next moment, young Mr. Crimper was striding toward them. "What *is* all this?" he demanded. "Why are you holding these kids?"

"We caught them in the act of robbing the store," Sergeant Molinson announced with pride.

"But we weren't!" Trixie cried. "Oh, Mr. Crimper, maybe you'll listen. You've *got* to listen! There's almost no time left!"

Quickly, Trixie told her story for the second time that evening. At the end of it, young Mr. Crimper looked appalled.

"*What*?" he gasped. "And *who* is the Midnight Marauder?"

Trixie told him.

After that, things moved more rapidly than Trixie would have believed possible.

Young Mr. Crimper insisted that the police should take immediate action. "If you don't," he said, "I'll make sure the story is given out to all the newspapers."

"And what a fine story it would make," a voice said softly.

Turning, Trixie saw the *Sun* reporter, Vera Parker, notebook in hand and ready to take down in shorthand everything that was said.

When Mr. Crimper pointed out that Sergeant Molinson could still arrest the three Bob-Whites if Trixie's theory was wrong, there was no more argument.

Soon Trixie found herself with Honey, Mart, and Reddy huddled in the back of a police car, speeding back along Glen Road.

"You wanna drop the dog off at your house?" the young policeman who was driving asked Trixie. He had a hopeful note in his voice, and he slowed down as he neared Crabapple Farm.

"No," Trixie answered firmly, her hand on Reddy's collar. "Something tells me that Reddy's going to be a big help—"

"For a change," Mart broke in, staring down at the dog. "He almost got me arrested."

"How is Reddy going to help us?" Honey asked.

Trixie sighed. "Up till now," she said, "no one has seen the Midnight Marauder except Lester Mundy—"

"And Reddy and Patch!" Honey exclaimed, her eyes wide. "And since Lester and Patch aren't here, that leaves only Reddy to identify the thief."

"I still don't understand," Mart said, shaking his head in puzzlement.

"Figure it out for yourself, Mart," Trixie said. "There is no way our suspect has ever seen Reddy—except on the night that Wimpy's was burglarized. I'm certain now that Reddy saw the thief hide the hamburger meat in that old shed. The Marauder didn't need it, you see, and couldn't afford to be caught with it. It would have been a dead giveaway. Reddy, on the other hand, thinks he's made a new friend—a friend who feeds him good, raw hamburger. That's why Reddy's been acting so nervous ever since that night. He's been waiting for his friend to show up with more meat! He's even been out searching for his new pal. Now, let's hope, he's going to identify that new pal in no uncertain terms."

"I still don't understand why the Midnight Marauder stole Celia's necklaces," Honey said thoughtfully.

"I wouldn't be surprised if those turn up soon, too," Trixie answered. "The Midnight Marauder had to make everyone think that all these robberies were the work of a teen-ager, so the only things taken, apart from small sums of money—"

"—were just window dressing," Mart finished. "Yes, I see it all now. Hey, Trix," he grinned at her, "I guess your brain isn't so pea-sized, after all."

Trixie bit her lip. "Don't say that, Mart," she said, her voice low. "I could still be wrong. Suppose the Midnight Marauder doesn't show up. Suppose—"

She was still worrying about it as the police car turned onto the Albany Post Road. It glided to a silent stop outside the tall Victorian house, hidden from view by some bushes. As it did so, three other police cars coasted to a quiet halt behind it.

Trixie had time to notice that Vera Parker, reporter's notebook in hand, had successfully begged a ride from Sergeant Molinson.

Now Vera Parker glanced at the three nervous Bob-Whites and said, "I know I owe you kids an apology. I'm sure now that I was wrong about what I wrote in my article. I think you kids are okay."

"Wow!" Mart breathed, as she hurried away. "And she doesn't even know yet whether Trixie's theory is right."

The wait seemed interminable. Twice, Trixie thought she saw the Midnight Marauder crouching low in the bushes of the front yard. Twice, it was only one of Sergeant Molinson's men. The rest were deployed around the remaining grounds.

At long last, their patience was rewarded. Slowly, a figure detached itself from the shadows and crept toward the house.

Honey gasped. "It's the Midnight Marauder!"

A warning pressure from Trixie's fingers on her arm silenced her.

The mysterious figure carefully placed something in a flower bed by a window. Then it cautiously broke a small pane of glass, unlocked and opened the window, and climbed inside. After what seemed like hours, the figure again appeared in the window. It climbed out onto the window-sill and dropped lightly to the ground. It carried a small sack clutched in one hand.

Placing it gently on the ground, the thief then reached down to the flower bed for the object hidden there.

Quickly the thief moved to a blank wall at the side of the house. The figure raised its arm. The nozzle of a paint can was ready to write its impudent message once more!

All this time, Reddy had been squirming and whining softly, while Trixie kept a tight grip on his collar. Suddenly Trixie let go of his collar, and he bounded from her side.

The three Bob-Whites had never seen him run so fast. With his long tail streaming behind him, he flung himself toward that figure, who was dressed in dark slacks and a lighter-tone shirt. The stillness of the night was shattered by Reddy's loud, joyous cries of welcome.

Trixie watched as he hurled himself into the totally unprepared arms of his new friend. Trixie had time only to feel a pang of sympathy for the figure, who was struggling to escape Reddy's slobbering kisses of welcome.

Then the police closed in, and the excitement was all over.

"This time we've *really* caught you, Midnight Marauder!" Sergeant Molinson announced, for the second time that evening. Then he couldn't resist adding—without looking at Trixie, "I knew it was you all along."

He snapped the handcuffs around two slim wrists and stared at his prisoner. The prisoner was—the antique dealer, Margo Birch!

Trixie had no chance to explain too much to the other Bob-Whites until after school the next day. Then they met in their clubhouse and listened quietly to all she had to say.

"Of course," Trixie finished, "Margo Birch was after those jewelry boxes all along. Most of them were junk—but one wasn't."

"The ballerina?" Honey asked.

Trixie nodded. "Yes, that's the one. Somehow Grandpa Crimper had managed to find one true work of art along with all the other junk he bought. Margo Birch recognized its worth as soon as she saw it. She's now told the police it's worth ten thousand dollars. It once belonged to a Russian empress, you see."

Brian was silent. He still regretted sleeping through the previous night's excitement. He had known nothing until Sergeant Molinson, personally, had escorted Trixie, Mart, Honey, and a disappointed Reddy to Crabapple Farm.

Honey stirred. "I'm glad I didn't really fib too badly to Miss Trask," she said, looking at Trixie.

"I *did* finish up spending the night with you, didn't I?"

Jim frowned. "All the same, Honey, I don't think you should do anything like that again."

Honey sighed. "No, you're right. It could have been a dangerous situation."

"How about you, Mart?" Di asked quietly. "Did everything work out okay at school?"

Mart smiled broadly. "Everything worked out just great!" he announced. "In fact, it couldn't be better. I had a long talk with my journalism teacher this morning, and you know what? He's let me off the hook. In the future, he's going to teach me how to write articles for the school paper—articles that *will* be published—"

"Once your spelling is corrected," Dan put in, grinning.

"And Miss Lonelyheart is going to retire," Mart said, sighing with relief. "At least, *this* Miss Lonelyheart is going to retire. It's a funny thing, though. The counselors at school got together and decided the column itself should continue, to offer help to anyone at school who needs it."

"But who's going to write it?" Di asked.

"One of the counselors," Mart told her. "Neat, huh? Now I don't have to worry about anyone."

Dan grunted. "Lester Mundy seems to have turned over a new leaf. His new club appears to have done him some good.

"Clubs are good," Dan said seriously, "as long as they're there to help people. The Bob-Whites always try to help someone in trouble. This time it was Mart. Next time"—he glanced at his friends—"it could be any one of us."

Di was still busy thinking. "What was all that business with the scrap of material that, at first, everyone thought was Reddy?"

"It was an important clue," Trixie explained. "It was torn from Margo Birch's shirt after she had damaged the school and then robbed Wimpy's. She went to hide the meat in the woods and tore her shirt on the way. Sergeant Molinson says that the scrap I had matched the tear in her shirt exactly. She was wearing the torn red shirt tonight. Probably the only thing she owns that isn't dressy!"

"And as for the truck," Mart added, "Margo Birch owned one similar to Crimper's—although it's hard to imagine her as a truck driver! If only we'd known."

Trixie sighed contentedly. "So it all ended happily. Dad and Moms are home safely and Moms's back is better."

"My parents are home, too," Honey said, "and was Celia ever glad to see Tom! They found the necklaces, by the way. Trixie was right again. The

Midnight Marauder had hidden them in the woods. The police found them this morning."

Trixie laughed. "Reddy's the only one who's unhappy now. He was hoping for more hamburger."

"But I'm not happy," Di announced. "*I* didn't get invited to the spring dance. I even wrote to Miss Lonelyheart about it."

Mart gasped. "Jeepers!" he exclaimed. "So you did! Consider yourself invited now. By me!"

Brian grinned at Honey. "How about it?" he said. "Will you be my date on Friday night?"

Jim smiled as his sister nodded shyly. "In that case, Dan," he said slowly, "that leaves only one female between the two of us."

Dan chuckled. "But I'm already booked," he said. "I'm taking Ruthie Kettner. I guess you're going to have to take Trixie yourself."

Jim smiled and leaned toward her. "What do you say, Trix? Will you come to the school dance with me?" His tone was light, but everyone could see that his eyes watched her closely.

Trixie's face flushed scarlet as she answered happily, "I'll be glad to go with you, Jim—unless another mystery comes along that I have to solve first."

The other Bob-Whites groaned in unison.

"Please—no more mysteries!" moaned Mart.

210

"At least, not until after the spring dance," added Jim. He smiled at Trixie, and she smiled back, her eyes shining. There would be more mysteries, she knew, but for now, the spring dance was enough to look forward to.